The Case of The Scream In The Smog
& Other Stories

T.G. Campbell

All characters in this collection of short stories are fictional. Any resemblance to persons living or dead is purely coincidental.

ALSO BY THE AUTHOR

Dedicated to Mum.

TABLE OF CONTENTS

ACKNOWLEDGEMENTS

Thank you to Christine Wagg, Historian at the Peabody Trust and co-author of *Homes for London: the Peabody Story* for her assistance. The book can be ordered from the Strathmore Publishing website www.strathmorepublishing.co.uk. Once there, click on 'store' to find details about *Homes for London: the Peabody Story* by Christine Wagg and James McHugh.

Thank you to my siblings, especially my eldest sister, for their continued support of my writing.

Thank you to Richard A. Boxshall and Kim J. Cowie for their enthusiasm for the Bow Street Society and ongoing support.

The Case of the Scream in the Smog

I

Mr O'Mooney wet his lips and grimaced. The rottenness
of sulphur mixed with the saltiness of tears filled his
mouth as dirt coated his tongue. Swallowing, he felt his
throat constrict in protest before a dry heave forced a large
globule of brown saliva from his lips. Holding his knees,
he spat out the remaining foulness, cleared his throat, and
pulled his scarf over his mouth and nose. As he then dried
his tears, his sore, red eyes gazed into the impenetrable
yellow smog that erased the cobblestones and deafened
him with its silence.

Where am I?

He glanced over his shoulder but saw only smog.

"Mercer Street," he said in a quiet voice. "Yeah…
must be."

He held out his hands and shuffled forward.

Suddenly, the toe of his boot struck something
hard, causing him to grunt in pain.

"Bloody smog," he muttered under his breath as
he used his foot to feel along whatever he'd kicked.
Assuming it to be the pavement's edge, he slid his foot
forward and felt more solid ground. Reassured, he stepped
onto it with both feet and held out his hands as he shuffled
forward once more.

Within moments, his fingertips felt a smooth, cold
surface. Holding his hands flat against it, he slowly slid
them downward until he felt a different texture. Tackier
than the first, it stretched out to the sides at a few inches
width. Coupling it with the smooth surface, he assumed he
was at a shop's plate-glass window. The parade of shops
he passed by daily on Mercer Street then sprang into his
mind's eye.

Cupping his hands against the glass, he rested his
face upon them and peered into the shop. Once his eyes

11

had adjusted to the gloom, he could see many silhouetted shoes placed upon stands of various heights and sizes.

Grant & Son, the cobblers.

A prickling sensation swept across his body at the realisation. Pulling back from the glass, he looked skyward and mumbled, "Thank you, God." A glance to the smog on his right, though, reminded him of the challenge still to come. "Not home yet, lad."

Keeping his palms close to the shop's facade, he side-stepped along it to its neighbour, and so on until he touched air. Finding the blunt corner of the rough brickwork, he shuffled around it to enter the next street before repeating his navigational method to find his way along it. When he felt air for a second time, he hesitated.

If this here's Shadwell High Street, I'm gonna have to cross the road. He felt the pit of his stomach tighten. *But if it's not…* "If it's not, I've still gotta keep goin'." A shiver coursed through his body. "Come on, lad." He stretched out his right arm and, resuming his side-stepping, felt along the ground with his foot until he came to the pavement's edge.

He stepped down onto the cobblestoned road and turned to his right.

"That's it, lad." He tentatively shuffled forward. "Just across 'ere." Feeling the toe of his boot nudge something hard, he then traced the pavement's edge with his foot before stepping cautiously onto it. As he did so, his shoulder encountered a lamp post that threatened to send him off balance. Swiftly gripping it with both hands, he clung onto the cold, damp metal as he tried to gather his bearings. *The lamp post must be on the corner.* He stepped around it and, holding it behind his back, took a few moments to consider his next move.

Eventually, he took a small side-step to the left and shuffled forward with his hands held out. For some time, he continued to touch air, his arms moving in all directions as he searched for something—anything—solid to cling onto. Finally, his boot struck something hard, prompting him to hurl himself at whatever it was he'd found. Feeling a sudden compression of his chest, followed by sharp stinging in his cheek, he realised he'd struck a brick wall. Clinging onto its rough edges, he pictured himself spread across it like a fly caught in a spider's web and smirked. "It's a good thing no one can see me."

A dog barked in the distance, thereby pulling Mr O'Mooney back to reality.

Feeling a newfound confidence in his route, he continued his journey up the street, around the corner, and along the next street. When he once again touched air, he felt his heart skip a beat.

Almost there…

He shuffled across the pavement, stepped down onto the cobbled road, and tentatively walked across Charles Place toward the gate to Peabody Square—or so he hoped.

"Who goes there?!" a man's voice yelled from the smog.

It was like warmth being poured onto Mr O'Mooney's numb ears. Rushing forward, he cried, "It's I, Mr Alan!"

"Mr O'Mooney?" Mr Alan enquired, stunned, as he materialised from the smog.

"Yes." Mr O'Mooney panted as he gripped the porter's shoulder. "Thank you, God, for seeing to my safe return."

Mr Alan's grey-green eyes were concerned as he watched him catch his breath. From behind a scarf, he stated, "I didn't expect you to return until the morning."

"It may as well be the time it has taken me to walk from the station." Mr O'Mooney wiped the sweat from his forehead with the back of his hand. "Is the gas lit?"

"Aye."

"Good. I've had my fill of stumbling around. I wonder how you can stand it all the night, Mr Alan."

"The smog hides the likes who've no business bein' 'ere, so someone's gotta be on the gate to keep 'em out. Superintendent Reid's decided that's me. The peace of mind and bit extra it gives puts me in no mind to complain, though." Mr Alan guided Mr O'Mooney through the gate. "Mind how you go, now. There'd be no hope of findin' you if you took a tumble."

"Thank you. Goodnight."

"Goodnight."

The dwellings in Peabody Square were housed within four detached, inwardly facing blocks to form a fragmented courtyard. Mr O'Mooney resided with his wife and children in the south block. Relying upon memory alone to guide him, he shuffled forward in a straight line from the gate until his hands felt the brickwork of the block's rear.

Once again, he kept his hands close to the wall as he side-stepped his way around the building to its front. In spite of the cold, he felt the tension in his body ease with each step. Visions of his wife holding a steaming bowl of stew by a roaring fire filled his mind's eye, quickening his pace.

The sound of sliding wood suddenly penetrated the near silence of the deserted square. Distinguishing the faint glow of the gas lamps on either side of the south block's main door, Mr O'Mooney pressed onward with little thought to what he'd heard.

"I shall never let you go," a man's voice said close by.

Almost there…

Yet, as Mr O'Mooney came within arm's reach of his destination, a terrifying scream sent him leaping backward into a stumble. Falling onto his coccyx, the horrific thud and violent crunch he heard a moment later cut short his sharp cry. Staring wide eyed into the smog, he felt his blood run cold.

II

Mr Bertram Heath's green eyes appeared to sparkle and gleam as his fingers drummed the doors across his knees. Painted black and varnished to a shine, the doors formed part of the two-wheeler hansom cab he travelled in. Gripping their edge, he half-stood from the narrow bench to peer over the brown mare at the road ahead. Sitting a moment later, he then pressed his face to the glassless window to his right before leaning across Dr Locke to peer through hers. Pressing her back against the seat, she warned, "You will injure yourself."

Mr Heath sat. "Begging your pardon, Doctor."

At twenty-five, he was the younger of the two by five years. At five feet three inches tall, he was also nine inches shorter. Whilst the cold wind whipped his short, light-brown hair, her long, dark-blonde hair remained motionless in its sculptured arrangement of tightly pinned curls. Their attires also formed a stark contrast; his coat, suit, and tie were shades of brown, whilst her tailored coat, knitted scarf, and smooth leather gloves were midnight blue, teal, and black respectively. The only similarities between them appeared to be their unblemished, fair complexions and slender builds.

"Is the impending investigation weighing upon your mind?" Dr Locke enquired.

"Not at all."

"Are you quite certain of that?"

Mr Heath smiled broadly. "Oh, yes."

"The details which Miss Trent gave us about Mr Alan's case were quite violent."

"Yes, they were." Mr Heath rummaged around in a brown paper bag. From it, he took a hard-boiled, cherry-flavoured sweet that he tossed into his mouth.

Dr Locke studied his expression for any hint of distress but found none. "It's simply that you have been restless since we left Bow Street."

Mr Heath paused in his sucking of the sweet. "Have I?"

"You have. Is it the smog?"

"The lifting of the smog *was* a *tremendous* relief," Mr Heath admitted as his tongue moved the sweet from one cheek to the other.

Since the early hours of the morning, a strong wind had steadily cleared the overbearing smog until, by mid-afternoon, it had gone. In its wake was intermittent yet light rainfall, with the temperature being only a fraction milder than they experienced the previous night.

Noticing the sign for Shadwell High Street, Mr Heath gripped the doors' top to lean out. With heartfelt glee, he exclaimed, "We're almost there!"

Dr Locke lofted a brow. "Your enthusiasm to see a dead body is disturbing."

Mr Heath's face blanched as he looked back at her and sat. "Oh no. No, it's not that at all. Oh my." He swallowed the last fragment of sweet.

Dr Locke knitted her brow, perturbed. "Then why are you so keen to get there?"

Mr Heath glanced at the road. "I suppose I should've explained. It's rather a failing of mine. I become so over-zealous, particularly when I'm passionate about something, and I forget that others might misunderstand my words, or intentions."

Dr Locke waited with expectant eyes.

"I've long held a desire to visit a Peabody dwelling, and Mr Alan's case is my first opportunity to do so."

"Might I presume your interest is born from your work as an architect?"

"It is," Mr Heath replied. "Peabody Square in Shadwell is a particularly fine example of what is, undoubtedly, the noblest of endeavours ever encountered in the business of designing and constructing domestic dwellings. As I'm sure you're aware, 'Peabody' refers to the wealthy American banker and philanthropist, Mr

George Peabody. His vision was to design and construct clean and affordable housing for London's artisan and labouring poor.

"It's a vision that has continued to be realised to this day through the good works of the Peabody Donation Fund. It met the original construction costs of Peabody Square when it was completed in 1866. Furthermore, the fund's board of trustees oversee the square's management, alongside that of the other Peabody estates."

"And being an architect, you appreciate the challenges which arise from such an endeavour," Dr Locke mused aloud.

"Indeed!" The broad smile returned to Mr Heath's face. "But my appreciation isn't limited to the bricks and mortar. Too many people in London are forced to live in squalid conditions through *no* fault of their own. They're even charged exorbitant rents for the so-called 'privilege!'" Striking the doors' edge with his fist, he then shook his hand to expel the subsequent pain. "I'm a *passionate* advocate for clean, honest housing for all, and the Peabody dwellings are *certainly* that. So much so that an 1885 parliament report recorded a two-year waiting list for tenants."

"Some of my poorest patients have mentioned such a list," Dr Locke remarked in a cool tone. "With a handful of those telling me they had been refused a place upon it because they were either unemployed or working on the markets at the time."

Mr Heath knitted his brow. "Hmm, yes, that *is* unfortunate." His brows lifted as he tilted his head and continued, "Although, the Peabody Donation Fund *does* rely heavily upon the rents paid by its tenants to meet the maintenance and salary costs of its various estates and the employees who manage them. Without such payments, I'm *certain* the fund would run dry. *Then* where would the tenants be? In the workhouse or worse, I'd wager."

The cab turned onto Charles Place, and the blocks of Peabody Square came into view.

"There it is!" Mr Heath exclaimed in delight.

As the cab slowed, Mr Heath flung open its doors and leapt from the vehicle.

"Watch how you go!" Mr Snyder called from the driver's seat.

Mr Heath appeared oblivious, though, as he gripped the wrought-iron railings and gazed up at the block with a soft gasp and widening eyes. His jaw remained slack as he looked from one architectural feature to the next, eager to commit them all to memory.

The block's English Bond brickwork was blackened by the soot-laden air with the occasional patch of yellow breaking through. A deep bracketed cornice adorned the top of the block's rear and side elevations, whilst tall, brick stacks protruded from its slated roof. Each of the block's five storeys above ground level were lined with a row of timber sash windows, behind which pristine net curtains were hung.

Awe inspired by the uniformity of the block's aesthetics, Mr Heath felt compelled to compare it to the square's other three. Therefore, without looking away, he moved along the railings toward the gate as Dr Locke alighted from the cab behind him. She saw a man emerge from the gate first. Unfortunately, she'd only gone as far as opening her mouth when the man intercepted Mr Heath and demanded, "Where do you think you're going?"

Mr Heath, noticing the sudden obstruction at the last moment, stopped dead in his tracks. Looking up into the newcomer's face, he saw grey-green eyes glaring out at him from behind a dark-brown scarf and hair. Placing his age in the mid-thirties, Mr Heath glanced over the man's rugged facial features and broad arms. Deciding that putting some space between them would be a sensible move, Mr Heath took a few steps back and held out his hand. "Mr Bertram Heath, architect and member of the Bow Street Society."

The man's glare softened. "You sent by Miss Trent?"

"We were," Dr Locke interjected as she joined them. "Doctor Lynette Locke. I, too, am a member of the Bow Street Society. I'm also a qualified medical practitioner with my own private practise."

The man looked at her warily before coming to a decision. At which point, he lowered the scarf from around his mouth to reveal a clean-shaven jaw and sideburns. In a more genial tone, he said, "Mr Keegan Alan. Sorry about before, sir. We get a lot of people trying to come in who've got no business to. They like to sleep in the passages, out of the cold." He then added under his breath, "And more."

"You're a porter here, aren't you?" Mr Heath enquired.

"Aye, working under Superintendent Dougal Reid for the board," Mr Alan replied.

"We understand from Miss Trent that one of your tenants heard a scream last night," Dr Locke began. "Followed shortly thereafter by the discovery of a woman's body. Is that correct?"

"Aye. We found her at the bottom of the stairs of the south block." Mr Alan thumbed over his shoulder. "But it weren't just Mr O'Mooney who heard the scream. I did, here at the gate, and some of the tenants in the other blocks come to the office this mornin' to ask what it was all about."

"We would like to see where Mr O'Mooney stood when he heard the scream, and where the woman's body was found, if we may?" Dr Locke enquired.

Mr Heath's eyes gleamed with excitement.

"If you must," Mr Alan replied.

Walking through the gate and around the south block, they entered Peabody Square. As Mr Heath had hoped, there were three additional blocks identical to the first. Clasping his hands together, he strolled to the centre of the yard and slowly turned on the spot to admire each of the blocks. "*Marvellous*, simply *marvellous*."

"Mr O'Mooney said he was by the door to the south block when he heard the scream," Mr Alan said, looking between them.

Waiting for a response from her fellow Bow Streeter, Dr Locke then cleared her throat to gain his attention. When this failed, she called, "Mr Heath, are you still here with us?"

"Pardon?" Mr Heath enquired as he was suddenly pulled from his reverie. Seeing Dr Locke and Mr Alan watching him, he realised one must've asked him a question. Having not the slightest idea of what it was, he requested, "Could you repeat that, please?"

"Are you still here with us?" Dr Locke enquired, placing a hand upon her hip.

"Yes," Mr Heath replied, hurrying back to them. "Yes, of course." He peered up at the south block. "How dense would you say the smog was here last night?"

"You couldn't see your hand in front of your face," Mr Alan replied.

"Mr O'Mooney was stood by the door when he heard the scream," Dr Locke informed Mr Heath who looked across the yard.

"Courtyards are *notorious* for being misleading when it comes to identifying the origins of a sound," Mr Heath said. "It's their shape. The sound sort of bounces around like a ball in a box. The gaps between these blocks would have lessened the effect but only by a small margin I'd wager." He turned to peer up at the south block once more. "No, the scream alone shan't tell us where it came from." He shifted his gaze to the others. "And the dense smog would've made it impossible for Mr O'Mooney, or anyone else, to see who'd screamed."

"Was anything else discovered, aside from the woman's body?" Dr Locke enquired.

"There was some blood in the yard," Mr Alan replied.

"May I see?" Dr Locke enquired.

Mr Alan led her to a spot several metres away. "Here."

Dr Locke leaned forward to take a closer look. "Where?"

"It ain't there now," Mr Alan replied. "I hosed the yard first thing this morning."

Dr Locke fixed him with a steely gaze. "To conceal the truth of the matter from the tenants?"

"Nah, to do what I was told," Mr Alan replied, irritated. "It's one of my duties."

Dr Locke's mouth formed a hard line as she strove to contain her displeasure. It was therefore with great tension in her voice that she enquired, "Can you recall if the amount of blood was closer to a thimbleful or a pint glass?"

"Pint glass," Mr Alan replied. "Maybe half-a-pint."

Dr Locke looked up at the block and thought aloud, "The location of the blood is consistent with someone falling from a height." She wrote down her best guess for the distance in her notebook. "One doesn't plummet like a stone, but rather tumbles like a rag doll."

"Blimey," Mr Alan remarked, turning a little pale.

"Where is her body now?" Dr Locke enquired.

"Mr Caulfield saw her taken to the hospital over on Glamis Road," Mr Alan replied with some reluctance.

"Is Mr Caulfield a porter, too?" Mr Heath enquired.

"No," Mr Alan replied, glancing away from them.

"He's a constable with the Metropolitan Police, correct?" Dr Locke enquired.

Mr Alan looked uneasily between them. "Aye."

"But as we weren't met by one of his senior officers, I presume Mr Caulfield was acting in his capacity as a tenant rather than a constable?" Dr Locke enquired.

Mr Alan folded his arms. "We all thought she'd fallen down the stairs. It weren't until we found the blood this morning that Mr Reid told me to fetch the Bow Street Society."

"I see." Dr Locke glanced at Mr Heath who stared at her in wonderment. "I've met Constable Caulfield once before. I've no interest in causing any trouble for him with his senior officers."

Mr Alan lowered his arms, but uncertainty remained in his eyes.

"*If* we discover the poor woman was a victim of murder, though, we shall be obliged to report our findings to the police," Dr Locke said.

Mr Alan's face contorted into a glare.

"*If*, on the other hand, we discover she was the unfortunate victim of an accident, then it shall be Miss Trent's decision as to whether we report the matter to the police," Dr Locke continued. "Do you understand?"

The tension eased in Mr Alan's face. Looking from Dr Locke to Mr Heath and back again, he considered her terms. Having met the clerk of the Bow Street Society that morning, he knew he could rely upon both her and the group's discretion. Nevertheless, he replied in a quiet voice, "I'll have to talk to Mr Reid about it."

"As is your right," Dr Locke agreed. "In the meantime, please show us precisely where the body was found."

Mr Alan glanced around and saw the yard was deserted. "This way."

The first area one came to upon entering the south block was a north-facing square entrance hall with a high ceiling. At the rear of the hall was an open doorway leading to a long corridor running from east to west. Beyond this was a set of steep, uncarpeted stairs. Their footsteps echoed as Mr Alan led them across the hall and through the doorway.

When they emerged into the corridor, the Bow Streeters saw a short passageway to the immediate right of the stairs. Previously obscured from view by the hall's rear wall, it had some steps leading down to a closed door.

After casting a cursory glance at the passageway, Mr Heath dismissed it in favour of the many wooden doors lining the corridor. Appearing to run for the block's entire length, the corridor had featureless, Alabastine painted walls, a flat, Jelstone White covered ceiling, and lit gas lamps at regular intervals. The only daylight came from the hall's open doorway.

"She was here." Mr Alan pointed to the foot of the stairs.

"Could you show us how she was lying, please?" Dr Locke enquired.

Mr Alan stared at her for a moment before giving a brief shake of his head, coupled with a soft sigh. He lay on his back upon the floor, rested his head on the bottom stair, and placed his left arm beside his head and his right upon his stomach. "She were like this."

"Thank you," Dr Locke said and allowed Mr Alan to stand. "Was she known to either you, Mr Caulfield, or Mr O'Mooney?"

Mr Alan shook his head. "She weren't a tenant."

"Perhaps she was a guest of one?" Mr Heath suggested.

"Could be," Mr Alan replied.

"Where does this door lead to?" Dr Locke enquired, indicating the door at the end of the short passage.

"Outside," Mr Alan replied. "It's locked in the winter."

Mr Heath rubbed his hands together and strolled to the cast end of the corridor. As he did so, he felt Mr Alan's gaze boring into his back. It unsettled the architect a little, especially since he hadn't the first idea about how to defend himself.

"Was there any blood on the stairs when you found the body?" Dr Locke enquired.

Mr Alan considered his answer and shook his head. "Not that I saw."

"Is Mr O'Mooney and Mr Caulfield at home?" Dr Locke enquired. "It would be helpful to speak with them."

"Mr O'Mooney is at the stables," Mr Alan replied. "He's a coachman for a family down Richmond way. Mr Caulfield is on duty somewhere."

Dr Locke frowned. "That's unfortunate."

Mr Heath strode back down the corridor toward them. "I don't suppose I could take a look at one of the dwellings?"

"No," Mr Alan replied, causing Mr Heath's face to droop.

"Aside from the scream, did Mr O'Mooney hear anything else?" Dr Locke enquired.

"A thud," Mr Alan replied. "And a man sayin' 'I'll never let you go,' or sumin' like that."

Dr Locke lofted a brow. "Such a statement wasn't concerning to you and Mr Caulfield?"

Mr Alan's features tightened. "She fell down the stairs."

"And yet blood was only found in the yard," Dr Locke pointed out.

"That could've been owt," Mr Alan countered.

"It could. But now, I must visit the hospital." Dr Locke headed for the entrance hall, prompting Mr Alan to narrow his eyes.

"I shall return as soon as I'm able," Dr Locke called. "Good day, gentlemen."

III

The Lockes had made charitable donations to the East London Hospital for Sick Children for some years. It was little wonder, then, that she had recognised it as the hospital on Glamis Road that Mr Alan had referred to. Within a comfortable walking distance of Peabody Square—even during a terrible smog—it had New Road to its left and Labour in Vain Street at its rear. Although its primary function was to care for seriously ill infants, the hospital also had a secondary function as a dispensary for women. Thus, it would've been a natural choice for Constable Caulfield when considering where to move the body.

Dr Locke loved the hospital building. Its archways and pointed gables adorned with crosses reminded her of a church, which, to her mind, was rather fitting since both were sanctuaries. As she looked upon the covered porch at the summit of the stone steps, and moved her gaze across the hospital's winged facade, she saw the establishment was set back from the pavement. Also the wings' arched windows overlooked a narrow yard below street level, as well as the wrought-iron railings marking the hospital's boundary. Finally, the words 'EAST LONDON HOSPITAL FOR CHILDREN,' chiselled into stone panels adorning the central wing and walls on either side, never failed to fill her heart with admiration.

Upon entering, Dr Locke was warmly greeted by a passing nurse. After exchanging pleasantries and giving a brief explanation for her visit, Dr Locke followed the nurse downstairs. When they reached their destination, the nurse politely requested Dr Locke remain in the corridor whilst she slipped into the room. A soft murmur of voices followed; the nurse's remained at a respectful volume, whilst the second—a man's—was elevated and irritable.

"Yes, send her in," the man's voice said through a sigh.

Dr Locke stepped back as she heard the nurse's approach.

"Doctor Greenwood will see you now, Mrs Locke," the nurse announced, opening the door wide.

Beyond was a low-ceilinged, windowless room with exposed brick walls and a stained stone floor. Several lit gas lanterns were suspended from an angular network of pipes running across the ceiling. A strong smell of chemicals laced with stale tobacco smoke filled Dr Locke's nasal passages as she entered. The scent reminded her of a certain Canadian's dead room. As did the trio of marble slabs lining its centre, all of which were occupied by bodies draped in stained sheets.

"That will be all," a tired-looking gentleman instructed the nurse. His pale-blue eyes followed her from the room before shifting to regard Dr Locke. He was in his early forties with unkempt, salt-and-pepper hair and matching mutton chops lining an angular jaw. The folds of his frock coat were stiff with a multitude of unidentifiable stains, whilst his off-white shirt and faded black trousers, waistcoat, and tie were pristine by comparison.

"I believe we've met before," Dr Greenwood stated.

"Once. When my husband and I were given the privilege of a tour."

"You must be one of our generous benefactors, then."

"Indeed, I am. The hospital's financial health isn't the focus of my visit today, however."

"If you were hoping for a peek at these unfortunate souls, you will be disappointed."

Dr Locke rested her hand upon the first slab. "I wish to examine the body of an unidentified woman brought here late last night by a tenant of Peabody Square in Shadwell."

"A tragedy." Dr Greenwood placed himself between Dr Locke and the slab. "She took a tumble down some stairs, or so I was told." He offered a genial, yet contrived, smile. "I still cannot permit you to look at her." His smile disappeared. "Irrespective of your assumption that your wealth gives you the right to do so."

"Not my wealth, my expertise."

Dr Greenwood furrowed his brow. "Expertise?"

"Yes, I'm a fully qualified doctor of medicine."

"Can a woman be fully qualified at anything?" Dr Greenwood sneered.

"Not only fully qualified but surpass her peers in the breadth of her knowledge and skill."

Dr Greenwood released a soft grunt of amusement.

"For example, were you aware that blood was discovered in the yard of Peabody Square?" Dr Locke enquired as she unfastened her coat.

The mirth vanished from Dr Greenwood's expression. "No." He folded his arms. "I'm not a surgeon investigating a crime, Mrs Locke."

"Doctor Locke—"

"I am an underpaid and overworked doctor of a glorified workhouse," Dr Greenwood interrupted with a raised voice. "She's one of hundreds who will be placed upon my slab. I've neither the time nor the resources to conduct a post mortem on all of them."

Dr Locke placed her gladstone bag on the slab. Putting on a leather apron she'd taken from it, she put it and her coat aside. "I'm not asking you to conduct post-mortems on them all; just one. Under my supervision."

"Now see here, Doctor—"

"What I see is a good man made cynical by his work."

Dr Greenwood's lips parted as the rest of him stilled.

"And a woman whose death is unexplained," Dr Locke continued. "I can at least do something about the latter." She glanced at his grim frock coat. "If you assist me, you may be able to amend the former."

Dr Greenwood perched upon the slab's edge, thereby closing the distance between them. His demeanour also calmed as he searched her eyes. In a soft tone, he enquired, "How did you come to hear of this poor woman's death? I thought Peabody dwellings were only for the poor."

"They are. I'm here as a member of the Bow Street Society. A porter at Peabody Square, Mr Alan, acting under the orders of the superintendent, Mr Dougal Reid, hired us to investigate the strange circumstance of her death and subsequent discovery of her body."

Dr Greenwood tilted his head as he folded his arms and rubbed his chin. He looked sideways at her. "Is there cause to believe it wasn't an accident, then?"

"That's what I hope to determine by conducting the post-mortem."

Dr Greenwood looked back at the slab's occupant as he considered the request. Eventually, he said, "Very well."

Facing the slab proper, he folded back the sheet to reveal the head and shoulders of a woman in her early twenties with curly, red hair. There was bruising around her eyes and a stain on her earlobe the colour of zinfandel wine. Grains of dirt also clung to her cheeks, eyelashes, and hair. Dr Locke retrieved a magnifying glass from her bag and studied the stain.

"I've seen this before; it's brain fluid." Dr Locke gently turned the woman's head and felt some resistance. Leaning closer, she studied what she could of the woman's vertebrae alignment without turning her over. "Her neck appears to be fractured in several places." She pushed aside the woman's matted hair and studied the base of her skull. "Her occipital bone also appears to be fractured. There is a deep wound here. The considerable amount of blood both in and around the wound, and in her hair, suggests it took some time for the heart to cease beating."

"She bled to death?" Dr Greenwood leaned in for a closer look.

"Possibly, but I would say either her broken neck, her head wound, or both, were the likeliest causes of her death. We can't be certain until we perform an internal examination of her spine and brain."

Dr Greenwood stood bolt upright. "Now?"

"Unless you have a prior engagement with another corpse?"

"No," Dr Greenwood mumbled.

"Good. Then let us begin."

IV

Mr Heath sucked upon a hard-boiled sweet as he studied the front elevation of the south block. Standing in the middle of the yard, he had a notebook and pencil and a furrowed brow. He recalled the architect Mr Henry Astley Darbishire had designed Peabody Square, along with several other estates for the fund. In his opinion, this fact was reflected in the uniformity of each block's architectural features. For instance, each window was perfectly aligned with the one above it. Yet, for all he admired Mr Darbishire's dedication to consistency, he found it impeded his efforts to isolate which window the woman could've fallen from.

"I tell you I heard her fall," Mr O'Mooney insisted. Standing in the clear daylight, he appeared to be in his mid-forties and approximately five feet six inches tall. His attire consisted of a knee-length, black cloak over brown trousers, jacket, and waistcoat. Black boots weighed down his feet but didn't detract from the impressiveness of his broad frame. His dark-grey, wavy hair was pushed back from his high forehead. Its limp, colourless appearance was in stark contrast to the intensity of his hazel eyes as he looked between Mr Alan and Dr Locke who stood with him to the left of the south block's main door. "I jumped back and heard the thud."

"You leapt *back* from the wall?" Mr Heath enquired in a light voice. Striding over to the block, he placed his hands upon its wall and looked upward. "Yes. Yes, I see now. The window must have opened somewhere *very* close above for you to feel the need to *leap*." He took a single jump back. "Out of harm's way."

Mr Alan grimaced as he recalled Dr Locke's description of how the woman would have fallen. Slipping his hands into his coat pockets, he hunched his shoulders and retreated to the door to look out across the yard.

"Mr O'Mooney, you didn't trip over the woman's body when you leapt—she would've fallen where the blood was, correct?" Mr Heath enquired.

"Yes," Dr Locke replied.

"Likewise, you didn't encounter any sign of her body on your return to the gate and Mr Alan," Mr Heath went on. "Therefore, we may eliminate the columns of windows directly in front and to the left of where you were standing. That just leaves the column to the right. Mr Alan, do all of these open?"

Mr Alan came away from the door and, shielding his eyes, peered up at the block. "The tenants on the first and third floors keep them closed on account of them having small children. The fifth floor's the laundry; no one's up there at that time of night."

"Which leaves the second and fourth floors," Mr Heath mused aloud.

"She had multiple fractures in her neck and a significant head wound," Dr Locke said. "The force of the impact was so severe, it crushed part of her skull. The bone fragments then compressed her brain, causing it to swell. Based upon its severity, I suspect it was more likely she fell from the fourth rather than the second floor."

Mr Alan once again slipped his hands into his coat pockets and moved away from the group to loiter in the south block's doorway, his complexion somewhat paler.

"Upon examining her clothes, I discovered a thick layer of dirt upon the heels of her shoes," Dr Locke continued. Walking over to Mr Alan, she waited for him to step aside before entering the entrance hall. "Did you mop the floor this morning?"

Mr Alan leaned through the doorway to glance over the floor. "Aye."

"Were there scuff marks or dirt upon it?" Dr Locke enquired.

Mr Alan met her gaze. "A few."

Dr Locke referred to her notebook. "Aside from a few coins and a tattered handkerchief, the contents of her pockets comprised of an old, faded set of rosary beads complete with a cross." She looked past Mr O'Mooney and Mr Heath, who stood behind Mr Alan, to the courtyard beyond. "Is the superintendent here?"

"He's gone to tell the board's secretary what's happened," Mr Alan replied.

"A pity." Dr Locke closed her notebook. "Never mind. Mr Alan, would you be so kind as to escort Mr Heath and me to the second-floor dwelling whose window is to the right of the main door?"

Mr Alan frowned as he looked from Dr Locke, to the stairs, and back again.

"I'll do it," Mr O'Mooney said, pushing his way inside.

"Come back 'ere," Mr Alan growled, pulling him back by the arm. "*I'll* do it."

"Then get on with it," Mr O'Mooney retorted. At Mr Alan's glare, though, he went back outside.

"This way," Mr Alan said. He led Dr Locke and Mr Heath to the second floor and, turning left, went across the corridor to knock on the first door he came to.

A baby cried in the distance, but they couldn't hear anything from within the dwelling.

Mr Alan pounded on the door. "Mr Grady? It's Mr Alan. I've got some people 'ere who want to talk to you."

The door behind them opened a crack. When Mr Heath looked over his shoulder, though, it slammed shut.

Footsteps approached from behind the door at which they stood. The sound of a key being turned in the lock then compelled the trio to step back.

"Sorry to disturb you, Mr Grady, but I've got Dr Locke and Mr Heath 'ere from the Bow Street Society," Mr Alan said as bloodshot eyes peered through the crack in the door. "May we come in?"

The room beyond was shrouded in gloom. Thus, few of the tenant's features could be distinguished in the dim gas light of the corridor. Yet, as the door opened wide and Mr Grady stepped outside, Dr Locke and Mr Heath could see he was in his early thirties with a grey and drawn complexion. His dark-brown waistcoat and off-white shirt were dishevelled, whilst his mousey-brown hair was unkempt. When he spoke, it was with a quiet, scratchy voice. He said, "I've been expecting you."

V

Dr Locke thanked Miss Trent as the clerk passed her some tea. Adding her own sugar and cream, Dr Locke took a sip and placed the cup and saucer upon the low table in front of her. She sat on the sofa in the Bow Street Society's parlour with Mr Heath beside her and Miss Trent in the armchair to the right of the fireplace. Dusk had fallen and with it had come fresh rainfall. Thus, the pitter-patter of rain interspersed the crack and pop of the roaring fire and the gentle flickering of the gas lamps.

"Mr Grady was beside himself with grief," Dr Locke informed Miss Trent.

"He and his common-law wife, Miss Elvina Newman, had been arguing about marriage," Mr Heath said. "Having been raised a devout Catholic, Miss Newman was keen to be wed, but Mr Grady wanted to wait until the Peabody Donation Fund granted him a larger dwelling."

"In time, the argument became heated, and Miss Newman opened the window," Dr Locke said. "She attempted to leave and, wanting to stop her, Mr Grady tried to take hold of her arm whilst telling her he'd never let her go. Unfortunately, when she tried to move away from his grasp, she lost her footing and toppled from the window. It was her scream the other tenants heard, and it was her body discovered at the bottom of the stairwell. I accompanied Mr Grady to the East London Hospital for Sick Children where he identified her."

"Why did he move her body if it was an accident?" Miss Trent enquired.

"He said he was worried others might think he had pushed her," Dr Locke replied. "Yet his biggest concern was people assuming Miss Newman had committed suicide. If they did, he knew she could never be buried on consecrated ground like she would've wanted. It was his last desperate attempt to protect the woman he loved."

Mr Heath's expression was sombre as he enquired, "What will happen now?"

"I shall discreetly inform Inspector Conway of our findings and allow him to quietly bring an official end to the matter," Miss Trent replied. "And a Catholic burial for Miss Newman."

"I certainly hope so," Dr Locke said. "I would hate for her to be remembered as simply the scream in the smog."

The Case of the Impossible Implication

I

In which the end is the beginning.

The low winter's sun poured through the icy window, casting its harsh white light upon a room Mr Virgil Verity felt he knew. Modest in size, it had dark varnished oak beams and panelling upon its walls. The latter of which had the coat of arms carved into it above the small stone fireplace. Ancient floorboards creaked under Mr Verity's feet as he peered through the window at the cobbled courtyard below.

Although he was entering the sixth decade of his life, Mr Verity felt like time had been rewound. The furniture, chosen for its practicality rather than style, consisted of a single bed, desk, and wardrobe. Pieces which reminded him of his own room during the brisk days of his late-thirties. Additions made to this room by its occupant were a large trunk with the initials 'D.W.' carved into its lid and an upright piano. Although he'd not been musically gifted, he recalled having to transport his own trunk on the back of a cart from the train station. His father's disapproval over his chosen profession had ensured his journey was the most tiresome it could be.

Catching sight of his reflection in the glass, he was reminded of time's relentless march. The rich brown of his beard, moustache, and hair had faded over the years, replaced by a washed-out off-white colour for the first two, and silver for the third. His once smooth, pink complexion had also become wrinkled and grey. Yet, even as his weakened spine caused him to stoop, and the cold caused his arthritic fingers to curl and ache, he still held the same passion for learning and zest for life as he had all those years ago. In short, he remained young in mind despite not being young in body.

Behind him, Miss Georgina Dexter lingered by the door with her dainty gloved hands clasped against the skirts of her forest-green, high-necked dress. Largely concealed by her midnight-blue, heavy winter coat, it hung a couple of inches off the ground. As a result, her laced, black-leather boots were visible, but not her ankles. Forty-two years younger than Mr Verity, she'd yet to experience all the joys and tribulations of life. Instead, her green eyes and unblemished complexion hinted at the naïve innocence that one could only experience during one's formative years.

Whilst the room brought memories to the forefront of Mr Verity's mind, it presented a portrait of its occupant in Miss Dexter's. Although she suspected the furniture had been supplied with it, the care with which it had been treated suggested a considerate nature. The upright piano was the most obvious sign of creativity, but more subtle ones were the handwritten musical scores littering the desk and peeking out from under the pillow. Ink bottles and pens had been strategically placed beside the bed and piano to ensure an idea could be recorded at a moment's notice. Crumpled balls of paper in the corner of the desk, and burnt fragments in the hearth, were remnants of those which hadn't satisfied the occupant's demanding standards. There were similar traces of rejected paintings in her studio at the Society's house.

Venturing further into the room, Miss Dexter went to the piano. Copies of *Illustrated Sporting and Dramatic News* and *Sporting Times*, and that year's *Racing Calendar*, were piled atop it. The last of which was open at that month's timetable, with many of the races annotated with the owner's notes. A cricket bat leaned against the corner beside the trunk, whilst a set of playing cards had been left upon the window's wide, stone ledge.

Tucked behind a clock on the mantel shelf were opened letters and a program for a Gilbert and Sullivan opera at the Savoy Theatre, London. Approaching the fireplace to examine it further, Miss Dexter changed her mind upon seeing an old newspaper beside it. Folded several times over, it held a highly praising review of a pianist's solo debut at the Theatre Royal, Drury Lane, in London. Recognising the pianist's name, she smiled.

"Forgive me, I had assumed he would be here," Mr Jeconiah Rogers said. Though older than Mr Verity by seven years, he shared his sentimentality about their surroundings. His blue eyes were also as keen as Mr Verity's brown in spite of his gaunt face. His once blond hair and sideburns, now light grey, had retained their natural curl. Attired in a dark-grey suit with matching waistcoat and tie, he also wore the recognisable black robe of Mr Verity's former profession. "Let us return to my office."

No sooner had the trio turned to leave, though, did a man in his early-forties stride into the room. Attired in the same style of suit as Mr Rogers, albeit dark brown in colour, he, too, wore the black robes Mr Verity was so familiar with. As before, Miss Dexter thought his bulbous nose was a perfect fit for his fleshy, rounded face. The shallow, narrow scratches upon his cheek, neck, and hand looked red and sore compared to when she'd seen them last. Yet, the bruise that covered his head's left side, temple, and cheek, continued to cause her the most concern. A portion of his thinning chestnut-brown hair was also matted where a deep gash marred his scalp's flesh. Though scabbed over, it remained horrific looking. Miss Dexter wondered how he could bare to stand with such an injury, let alone conduct his usual work as his appearance suggested he was.

Coming to an abrupt halt, the man looked at Mr Verity and Miss Dexter with raised brows before addressing Mr Rogers. "How unexpected." He cast a questioning look amongst them. "Am I interrupting?" He offered a contrived smile. "Forgive my boldness but," he gathered up the piles of publications from the piano, "I hadn't thought to find guests in my room."

"This is Mr Verity and Miss Dexter from the Bow Street Society," Mr Rogers said.

"Good afternoon," the man greeted with a polite smile.

"Sir," Mr Verity greeted in a northeast English accent.

"It's a delight to meet you in more pleasant circumstances, Mr Waller," Miss Dexter said with a dip of her head. "Miss Trent *will* be pleased to hear you're safe and well." She beamed at him, her eyes bright with relief.

"Miss Trent?" Mr Waller furrowed his brow. "That's not a name I'm familiar with."

"Now do you understand my reluctance?" Mr Rogers enquired from the Bow Streeters. "Mr Waller is not a well man."

"I'm in *perfect* health," Mr Waller said, affronted.

"Not for much longer," a man in his late-thirties warned as he suddenly stepped into the room. Dark-brown, almost black, sideburns snaked their way along his square jaw, thereby further elongating his already narrow face. The battered appearance of his cap matched the poor condition of his washed-out blue overcoat, brown cotton trousers and waistcoat, grey shirt, and dark-green tie. His black-leather boots were scuffed and caked in mud, with the stitching on the sole of one having come away at the toes. His fair complexion was also smudged with dirt, whilst his small, brown moustache was as unkempt as his hair.

A long, wooden club was in his right-hand, the index finger of which was largely missing.

Miss Dexter gasped and gripped Mr Verity's arm. With wide, terrified eyes, she whispered, "It's *him*!"

II

In which questions are asked.

"Why aren't you in the gatehouse, Mr Cantrell?" Mr Rogers demanded as the man entered his office.

In his early-fifties, Mr Cantrell was approximately five feet tall with spindly arms and legs, pointed nose, and receding black hair. His complexion was weathered, whilst his red nose denoted the copious amount of alcohol he habitually consumed for medicinal and relaxation purposes. His attire was a uniform of black frockcoat over a matching waistcoat, trousers, and cravat, a brilliant white shirt, and black-leather shoes shined to a polish. Grey, woollen fingerless gloves and scarf kept the cold at bay— aside from the flask of brandy in his pocket, that is.

Carrying a lantern, he held it aloft as he bowed low in front of Mr Rogers' desk. "Begging your thousand pardons, Headmaster, but I thought I ought to fetch them to you without delay."

Mr Rogers stood. "Fetch whom?"

Mr Cantrell stepped aside.

"Mr Virgil Verity, a retired schoolmaster, and Miss Georgina Dexter, an artist," Mr Verity announced as he entered arm in arm with his friend. "We are here as members of the Bow Street Society."

"Return to the gatehouse," Mr Rogers ordered.

Mr Cantrell bowed low a second time and, walking backwards into the corridor, closed the heavy oak door with a thud that reverberated around the room.

Of considerable size, it had a vaulted stone ceiling with dark-oak panelling covering its walls. On the left-hand side of the room was an impressive stone fireplace with a traditional log fire burning within it. The portrait of a middle-aged man in black robes hung from its wide chimney breast. Assuming it to be the founder, Miss Dexter observed how his eyes and slight lift of his mouth hinted at a benevolence his otherwise stern expression hid.

Aside from Mr Rogers' desk that stood before dual-latticed arched windows, the furniture consisted of several bookcases, an uncomfortable-looking chair reserved for students, and a grandfather clock. Stone busts depicting William Shakespeare, Aristotle, and Queen Victoria, amongst others, lined shelves on either side of the door.

"I'm Mr Jeconiah Rogers, the headmaster here. This is a respectable institution. There are no scandals or crimes for the Bow Street Society to investigate."

"I'm well-aware of your exemplary reputation," Mr Verity said. "And we're not here to start a scandal or investigate a crime."

"Then you have no reason to be here," Mr Rogers stated.

"Pardon me, sir." Miss Dexter cleared her throat. "But we do." She approached the desk and, with a slight bowing of her head, continued in a meek voice, "We wish to call upon one of the schoolmasters here—Mr Dominic Waller. I-I have a sketch of him." She retrieved it from her satchel and held it out to him.

Mr Rogers' eyes and lips twitched with recognition upon seeing the face. "Why?"

Miss Dexter withdrew her hand. "We're concerned for his welfare, sir."

"Are you friends of his?" Mr Rogers enquired, his hard tone and expression softening.

"I'm afraid not." Miss Dexter momentarily downcast her eyes before insisting, "But we're still worried about him." She grimaced. "He was in *such* distress after what happened."

Mr Rogers lifted his chin as he enquired in a curious tone, "You know of that, then?"

"He told us of it," Miss Dexter replied.

Mr Rogers lowered his chin and, turning his head away, mumbled, "He must be making a swifter recovery than we'd thought, then."

"May we see him?" Miss Dexter enquired with hopeful eyes.

Mr Rogers looked at her sharply. "See him?" He moved around the desk. "Why do you need to see him, if you're already aware of the situation?"

Miss Dexter looked to Mr Verity for assistance.

"He was hurt when he left the Society's house yesterday," Mr Verity replied.

"The Society's house?" Mr Rogers enquired, surprised. "I see." He furrowed his brows. "Then we have been speaking at odds." He headed for the door. "In which case, it would be impossible for you to see Mr Waller. Rest assured, though, he is as safe and well as can be expected under the circumstances."

"With all due respect, Headmaster, we'd like to see for ourselves," Mr Verity said as he and Miss Dexter turned toward him.

"To be able to put mine and Miss Trent's minds at ease," Miss Dexter added.

"Who is Miss Trent?" Mr Rogers enquired.

"Clerk of the Bow Street Society," Mr Verity replied. "We won't be long. You have my word."

Mr Rogers frowned. "He shan't know you."

"Not me, no, but he should recognise Miss Dexter," Mr Verity said.

"You don't understand." Mr Rogers' frown deepened. "But… very well. Seeing is believing, or so I am told." He opened the door. "This way."

III

In which the visitors arrive.

Miss Dexter slid her hands deeper into the fur muff resting upon her knee as she pressed her back against the seat. Although largely shielded from the wind by the side and rear walls of Mr Snyder's cab, the cold air nonetheless entered its open front and swirled around its interior. Thus, the tip of her nose and cheeks were a deep shade of pink. The former also threatened to drip, thereby obliging her to dab at it from time to time with her handkerchief.

In contrast, Mr Verity appeared unaffected by the inclement conditions. Instead, he sat beside her, studying her sketch, as leisurely as if he were on the beach at Brighton. She suspected his resilience was due to being raised in County Durham. Her Pa-Pa had often told her "the north" was cold, damp, and "miserable." Granted, "the north" was anywhere north of London according to her Pa-Pa, but she was adamant bad weather wasn't exclusive to the south.

"A bad to-do all round," Mr Verity mused aloud. "It's a shame he turned you down."

"Miss Trent and I were most distressed by it." Miss Dexter felt her cheeks warm. "Well, *I* was. Miss Trent was her usual calm self. I had wanted to run after him to insist upon an examination by Dr Locke. Miss Trent was quite right, though; we had neither the right nor the resource to detain him." Miss Dexter looked through the small, square hole in the cab's roof and gave Mr Snyder a warm smile when their eyes met. "If Mr Snyder had been there, Mr Waller might have been persuaded to stay." She returned her gaze to Mr Verity. "I *do* hope he is here."

"If he was wearing a black-and-purple striped tie, I'm sure of it." Mr Verity passed the sketch back to her, and she slipped it into her satchel. "I remember when I was a schoolmaster, the boys' uniform had dark-grey

43

blazers and a different-coloured tie for each House. Plato House had dark blue, Socrates House had burgundy, Aristotle House had dark green, and Epicurus House had pale blue. The colours of the school crest." He momentarily leaned forward to look out as they turned onto a dirt road. "I dined at the house of the headmaster of Hampstead Public School once. When I was being walked through the grounds, I saw some of the boys wearing the black-and-purple tie."

After a few minutes, a high stone wall emerged from the dense trees to the left of the road. Stained a dark brown at its base where the stone had absorbed the ground water, it otherwise had the appearance of a fortress wall but without the battlements.

The cab continued onward until, eventually, the dual turrets and wide arch of a gatehouse broke the bland structure. As they drew near, Mr Snyder pulled upon his horse's reins, and the animal slowed to a trot before coming to a halt at his instruction a few yards from the gate. Peering through the hole in the cab's roof, he touched the brim of his hat and said, "I'll be waitin' 'ere for you."

"Thank you, Sam." Miss Dexter smiled. She unlatched the doors and, flipping them open, stepped from the vehicle onto the frozen ground. Filling her lungs with the crisp, fresh air, she then released it with a weak smile. Whilst she relished the opportunity to be in the countryside, her concern for Mr Waller far outweighed her desire to savour her surroundings. Catching movement in the corner of her eye, she looked to a man loitering by the wall. His battered cap and clothes were as dirty as his face, suggesting he was a vagrant. Feeling a deep sympathy for his plight, she rummaged around in her skirts' concealed pocket for her purse.

"Leave 'im be, lass," Mr Snyder warned when she'd retrieved it.

Miss Dexter pursed her lips and knitted her brow as she returned her gaze to the vagrant. He was now walking away in the opposite direction, glancing

44

repeatedly over his shoulder as he went. Feeling ashamed for not offering him a shilling or two, she concluded Mr Snyder must've thought him a thief or other such unsavoury character.

"He's wasting his time," Mr Snyder remarked as he joined her. "Places like this aren't known for their charity to the poor."

"You can't leave that there," Mr Cantrell declared as he emerged from one of the turrets and strode toward Mr Snyder. "This 'ere's private property."

"Of Hampstead Public School?" Mr Verity enquired.

"It is," Mr Cantrell replied. "Is this cab yours?"

"It's mine," Mr Snyder replied.

"We travelled here in it, yes," Miss Dexter added.

"And we're going to travel back in it, too," Mr Verity said.

"Then do so," Mr Cantrell headed back toward his turret.

"We can't," Mr Verity said. "Not yet."

Mr Cantrell spun around and strode over to them. "Don't you know how *cold* it is?" He held up his red fingers. "How *frozen* my poor, old body is out here?" He put his hands together as if praying. "Please, leave, so I may warm myself by the fire."

"We're from the Bow Street Society," Mr Verity said. "I'm Mr Virgil Verity and these are my associates: Miss Georgina Dexter, an artist, and the driver is Mr Sam Snyder. I'm a retired schoolmaster and spiritualist."

"We've got no ghosts 'ere," Mr Cantrell said.

"We want to call upon the living," Mr Verity said.

"Mr Dominic Waller," Miss Dexter interjected.

"Do you know him?" Mr Verity enquired.

Mr Cantrell tilted his head back. "I might. He won't be expectin' you, though."

"No, we didn't make an appointment," Miss Dexter said, somewhat sheepishly.

"Wouldn't of mattered if you had," Mr Cantrell said.

"I don't understand," Miss Dexter said.

Mr Cantrell considered his options.

"Wait 'ere," he said after a few moments of deliberation. Returning to the turret to retrieve a lantern, he then unlocked the gates and opened them wide. "You'd best come with me," he told Mr Verity and Miss Dexter. "The stables' through there, to the right," he called over to Mr Snyder whilst pointing through the gloomy gatehouse. Upon seeing him touch the brim of his hat in acknowledgement, Mr Cantrell instructed Mr Verity and Miss Dexter, "Stay close and don't dawdle."

"We understand," Miss Dexter agreed.

Mr Cantrell led them through the gatehouse into a vast courtyard framed by medieval buildings, some of which had open-arched doorways to other areas. In its centre was a lush green lawn with wide gravelled paths on two sides. Leading the Bow Streeters along the first of these at a brisk pace, Mr Cantrell occasionally glanced back to ensure they hadn't strayed. Upon reaching the end, he unlatched a heavy oak door and took them into a long, candlelit corridor with a barrelled ceiling and tiled floor. Its pillar-lined left side overlooked a cobbled courtyard, whilst its stone-walled right side was littered with deep, narrow alcoves housing tall lanterns. Following the corridor around to the right, Mr Cantrell then took them down a second before stopping at a second oak door. To its right was a wooden plaque with the word 'Headmaster' written upon it.

Knocking thrice, Mr Cantrell waited to be invited in before unlatching the door and stepping inside.

IV

In which the Society become involved.

The aroma of tea filled the air as Miss Dexter poured the dark liquid into two cups. The warmth and crackle of the fire, coupled with the pitter-patter of rain against the kitchen window, made her feel at ease. Since establishing her artist's studio at the Society's house, it had truly become a home away from home. Yet, unlike the one she shared with her parents, she was at liberty to paint, sculpt, and experiment with photography for as many, or as few, hours as she wished. She also had the joy of Miss Trent's company for afternoon tea whenever the opportunity arose. Adding the cream and sugar to taste, she first served the clerk her drink before partaking of her own.

"How is your painting coming along?" Miss Trent enquired, stirring her tea.

"Well, thank you," Miss Dexter sipped from her cup and replaced it upon its saucer. "I believe it will be finished by tomorrow."

"Excellent." Miss Trent's face lifted with her smile. "All we need to do now is find a gallery willing to exhibit your work under the monocle of Georgina Dexter instead of George."

Miss Dexter hummed. "I'm afraid such a place doesn't exist."

Jolting in her chair as something suddenly banged against the window, she then clapped her hand over her mouth as she saw a man looking in at them. In his mid-forties, he had an horrific bruise on the left side of his face and scratches upon his cheek, neck, and hand. Water poured from his nose, chin, and ears as he repeatedly struck the glass with his fists. "*Help me, please!*"

Miss Trent leapt to her feet and, unbolting and unlocking the door, ushered him inside. Casting a worried glance over his dishevelled appearance, noting his unusual purple-and-black striped tie as she did so, she enquired, "What's happened? Are you hurt?"

The man half-stumbled to the table and, putting his hands flat upon it, bent over as he fought to catch his breath. "A-A man … attacked me … I ran … here."

Miss Dexter prepared a cup of sweet tea for him.

"Please, sit," Miss Trent invited, pulling a chair away from the table.

Dropping onto it like a sack of potatoes, the man accepted the offered teacup with trembling hands. "Th-thank you." He drained its contents and returned it to Miss Dexter who prepared him some more. "F-Forgive me for intruding upon you like this, ladies. I … I just ran and… I climbed over the wall, thinking it led into the street." He turned in his chair to peer through the window at the barren yard beyond. "Then I saw you sitting here…" He accepted the second cup of tea and sipped at its contents. "Y-You must think me a frightful sight."

Miss Trent and Miss Dexter sat opposite him.

"What is your name?" The former enquired. "I'm Miss Rebecca Trent, and this is Miss Georgina Dexter."

"Mr Waller," the man replied, putting the cup down. "Mr Dominic Waller." He glanced around, seemingly noticing his surroundings for the first time. "You live here alone?"

"No, this is the house of the Bow Street Society," Miss Trent replied. Granted, she *did* live there alone, but she wasn't about to reveal such a sensitive piece of information to a stranger who'd banged on her window mere moments before. "I'm its clerk, and Miss Dexter is a member."

"Oh…" Mr Waller offered Miss Dexter a polite smile. "Pleased to meet you."

Miss Dexter gave a brief dip of her head. "And you, sir."

"Where were you attacked?" Miss Trent enquired.

Mr Waller drank some more of his tea, the trembling in his hand having now eased. "By Covent

Garden Market. He came from nowhere and demanded money from me. I told him, in no uncertain terms, that I had none. Yet," he swallowed hard, "he insisted I give him some and tried to take a hold of me, scratching me in the process. I fought him off and ran."

"What did he look like?" Miss Trent enquired.

"I-I don't know. It all happened so quickly but," Mr Waller considered a moment, "Yes, the finger on his left hand was almost gone."

Miss Dexter stood. "I'll fetch my sketchbook so I may draw his likeness under your direction."

"Then I shall walk with you to the police station," Miss Trent said. "They may be able to find him if he's still in the area."

Mr Waller lofted his brows. "The police?" He vehemently shook his head. "No. No, that shan't be necessary." He stood, prompting Miss Trent to do the same. "I'm sure he has gone by now. Thank you for your help. I shan't forget it."

"But what if he hasn't?" Miss Trent enquired, deeply concerned. "He could be waiting for you in the street."

Mr Waller looked to the kitchen door and frowned deeply. Yet, a moment later, he gave a dismissive shake of his head. "No, I'm *certain* he would've gone by now. Just show me out, and I shan't trouble you any longer."

"It's no trouble," Miss Dexter said. Noticing the gash upon the side of his head, she frowned deeply. "One of our members is a doctor, she could—"

"*No!*" Mr Waller cried. "No doctors!" His desperate gaze darted from Miss Dexter, to Miss Trent, and the door. "*Please*. I just want to leave."

Miss Trent pursed her lips and released a deep breath through her nose. Unfortunately, there was only her and Miss Dexter in the house. Suspecting he was a man of considerable strength, she doubted they could detain him even if they tried. "Very well," she agreed, albeit with great reluctance. "Follow me, please."

49

V

In which the beginning is the end.

"This is Mr Verity and Miss Dexter from the Bow Street Society," Mr Rogers said.

"Good afternoon," the man greeted with a polite smile.

"Sir," Mr Verity greeted in a northeast English accent.

"It's a delight to meet you in more pleasant circumstances, Mr Waller," Miss Dexter said with a dip of her head. "Miss Trent *will* be pleased to hear you're safe and well." She beamed at him, her eyes bright with relief.

"Miss Trent?" Mr Waller furrowed his brow. "That's not a name I'm familiar with."

"Now do you understand my reluctance?" Mr Rogers enquired from the Bow Streeters. "Mr Waller is not a well man."

"I'm in *perfect* health," Mr Waller said, affronted.

"Not for much longer," a man in his late-thirties warned as he suddenly stepped into the room. Dark-brown, almost black, sideburns snaked their way along his square jaw, thereby further elongating his already narrow face. The battered appearance of his cap matched the poor condition of his washed-out blue overcoat, brown cotton trousers and waistcoat, grey shirt, and dark-green tie. His black-leather boots were scuffed and caked in mud, with the stitching on the sole of one having come away at the toes. His fair complexion was also smudged with dirt, whilst his small, brown moustache was as unkempt as his hair.

A long, wooden club was in his right hand, the index finger of which was largely missing.

Miss Dexter gasped and gripped Mr Verity's arm. With wide, terrified eyes, she whispered, "It's *him*!"

"How the *Devil* did you get in here?" Mr Rogers demanded.

"I come in through the gate, didn't I?" the man replied with a sideways glance at Mr Verity.

"You must have done so when Mr Snyder drove in," Mr Verity said.

"I did," the man smirked. "Thanks for that."

"Who are you?" Mr Waller demanded. "What do you want from me?"

The man lifted his club as he advanced upon the group, obliging them to retreat further into the room. "Sid David," the man replied. "You owe me money, Dom."

"He is the man who attacked you!" Miss Dexter cried.

"*Attacked* me?! *When*?!" Mr Waller exclaimed, shocked.

"Yesterday, back in London," Mr David replied, moving closer still. "Don't tell me you've forgotten me already."

"He has," Mr Verity said.

"Don't give me that," Mr David said, looking at him sharply. As he then lifted the club to point it at Mr Waller, though, Mr Rogers snatched it from him. "Oi! Give that back!"

Mr Rogers slipped it behind his back and retreated into the corner. "Not until you've heard what we have to say."

"What is going on?" Mr Waller demanded. "Who *are* you people?" He looked to Mr Verity and Miss Dexter. "And *you*," he looked at Mr David, "I don't know you from Adam."

"That's because you don't remember him," Mr Verity said. "Correct me if I'm wrong, Mr Rogers, but Mr Waller's had an accident recently, hasn't he? That's what caused the gash on his head."

Mr Rogers straightened and, with a sombre expression, replied, "Yes. He was knocked down by a coach and horses."

"And since then, he's not been able to remember much information, has he?" Mr Verity enquired. "And has become confused besides. He's not a schoolmaster here, is he?"

"No," Mr Rogers replied.

"Don't be *ridiculous*," Mr Waller said. "I've taught here for *years*."

"You were a student here for years," Mr Verity said. "That tie of yours is worn by the students, not the schoolmasters."

Mr Waller glanced down at the tie, confused.

"This proves it," Miss Dexter retrieved the newspaper from the mantel shelf and showed it to him. "See? Here's your name. You performed at the Theatre Royal, Drury Lane, to great acclaim. You're a highly talented pianist and composer."

"But I... I don't remember," Mr Waller said, taking it from her and staring at it, dumbfounded.

"You can't, not at the moment," Mr Rogers said. "You can remember some conversations, information from years ago—even if it is a little confused—but you seem to forget recent events after just a day."

"'E don't remember 'e owes me money, then?" Mr David enquired.

"No," Mr Verity replied.

"What does he owe you money for?" Mr Rogers enquired.

"Gamblin' debts," Mr David replied.

"The notes on the Racing Calendar," Miss Dexter mused aloud.

"And I'm still owed it, if he remembers it or not," Mr David pointed out.

"The Bow Street Society shall settle all debts," Mr Verity said. "And provide the expertise of a doctor who specialises in illness of the mind free of charge. Hopefully, in time, you'll get your memories back and be able to hold onto them, Mr Waller."

"I sincerely hope so," Mr Rogers said, sadly.

Mr Waller sat on the bed, staring at the newspaper in shocked silence.

"We'll ask Miss Trent to send the doctor to you, sir," Miss Dexter told him with a glance at Mr Rogers.

"It's time we went," Mr Verity said. "Come on, Mr David. We'll drive you back to London."

Mr David nodded and, studying Mr Waller's face for a few moments, frowned deeply. "Poor bloke," he muttered as he left, meaning every word of it.

The Case of the Lyall Lighthouse

I

Dr Percy Weeks hadn't left England since his arrival from Canada in 1893—until now. If he'd been asked about his next destination then, he would've said France or the United States of America. Scotland, specifically a desolate spot on its west coast, wouldn't have entered his thoughts. It hadn't entered his thoughts now, not as a vacation destination, anyway. It had been a letter from Bow Street Society clerk Miss Trent that had led him from his domain of the dead room and the familiar sights and smells of his haunts in London. It read:

> *Dear Dr Weeks,*
>
> *The Bow Street Society requests your assistance on behalf of Superintendent Mungo Roy of the Northern Lighthouse Board in Scotland, to investigate the disappearance of Occasional Lightkeeper Eòghann Stewart. Mr Stewart went missing from his station at the Lyall Island Lighthouse a week ago, with no sightings of him being made since. Given the lack of information about the potential causes of Mr Stewart's disappearance, the NLB wishes to keep the matter confidential until evidence of Mr Stewart's whereabouts can be presented to its board and, eventually, the public.*
>
> *You and I know discretion isn't one of your strengths, but we would appreciate it if you could endeavour to be on this occasion. The practise may even do you some good once you're back in London—hopefully. Please confirm in the usual manner of either your acceptance or declination of this assignment.*

If it's the former, Mr Skinner and Mr Heath will be waiting for you at the ticket office of St. Pancras Railway Station at four thirty this evening. You will travel on the five twenty-seven sleeper train to Dumfries, and then onto Cutcloy. Superintendent Roy is scheduled to meet you at the Banshee Inn, near the harbour, in two days' time to brief you further. Please, ensure you pack enough warm clothes for at least a week.

Sitting in a ragged armchair, Dr Weeks knocked back glass after glass of whisky poured from a bottle on the table. All the while, he listened to the rain beating against the window, the rumble of thunder directly overhead, and the crackling of the fire in the open hearth. If he listened carefully, he could also hear waves crashing against the shore in the distance. Although he was only twenty-nine, Dr Weeks' pallid complexion and bloodshot, dark-brown eyes made him appear tired and worn. His unkempt black hair and small moustache echoed the slovenly appearance of his clothes; faded brown cotton trousers, heavy, black leather boots, and old dark-green jumper. The jumper, hand-knitted in the traditional Gansey pattern, would've been at home on a fishing boat but looked out of place on the alcoholic.

Tossing back his latest shot of Scotch whisky, he rested the empty glass on his stomach as he looked across to Mr Callahan Skinner opposite. The retired Royal Navy officer was impeccably attired in a new rolled-neck navy-blue woollen jumper, thick black trousers, and sturdy boots. His close-cut brown hair was flecked with grey, whilst coarse brown stubble covered his upper lip and chin. Almost a decade older than Dr Weeks, Mr Skinner had a confident air born from life experience. The burn scars across the right side of his jaw and cheek, and his false right hand, were further testament to his quiet strength of character. Resting his left arm upon the chair's, a glass of porter in his hand, Mr Skinner gazed into the fire, lost in thought.

The sound of a page turning pulled Dr Weeks' gaze to Mr Bertram Heath sitting in the corner of the room to the right of the window. The architect was younger than Dr Weeks by only four years, but his boyish features meant he could've easily passed as his son. Attired in a burgundy woollen waistcoat with matching cotton tie, white shirt, and dark-brown suit, he had evidently ignored Miss Trent's warning about packing warm clothes. A brown overcoat, at least a size too big, was draped over his shoulders as he leaned toward the fire, a book held between his knees. His green eyes were infused with enthusiasm as he read the words, whilst loose strands of his light-brown hair fell about his face. Although Dr Weeks couldn't see the title, he knew it was *Treasure Island* by Robert Louis Stevenson because Mr Heath had "regaled" them with his knowledge of that author's connection to the Northern Lighthouse Board. He was the son of a former owner or something. Dr Weeks neither remembered nor cared.

The Banshee Inn was a short walk from the harbour at Cutcloy. Despite the so-called 'arrangement' made between Miss Trent and Superintendent Roy, the latter had yet to appear. They were already entering their second evening in Scotland and had seen neither hide nor hair of their elusive client. The innkeeper had cited the bad weather as the likeliest reason for the delay, since Cutcloy was at the end of a long dirt road that had been turned into a quagmire by the incessant rain. This, and the fact Dr Weeks was obliged to rely on his fellow Bow Streeters to translate the innkeeper's words due to his thick accent, meant Dr Weeks was reaching the end of his tether.

The inn's front door flew open.

All at once, Mr Skinner sat bolt upright and put down his glass before resting his actual hand upon the butt of the revolver tucked into his belt. Mr Heath also dropped his book and scrambled to pick it up, whilst Dr Weeks watched a tall figure enter and stride toward him.

They wore a black trilby hat and scarf covering the lower half of their face; both were swiftly removed once the innkeeper had secured the door. Beneath was the smiling face of a fair-skinned gentleman in his early forties with smooth cheekbones and neat, yet damp, dark-brown beard, moustache, and hair. The bright blue of his eyes appeared vivid in the firelight as he regarded each of the Bow Streeters in turn. Relieving himself of his sopping great coat and passing it to the innkeeper to hang by the fire, he adjusted the damp cuffs of his double-breasted dark-blue suit and smoothed down its lapels. His trousers were also damp, their darkened material clinging to his shins as he took a seat by the fire.

All the while, Mr Skinner kept his hand upon the gun. He and Dr Weeks exchanged sideways glances when the newcomer passed them. Mr Heath held his book firmly against his chest.

The cacophony of sounds caused by the storm momentarily filled the room.

The newcomer glanced skyward, then out the window.

Dr Weeks poured more Scotch whisky into his glass. When the newcomer met his gaze as a result, he remarked, "Yer late." He put the bottle down with a thud and held the glass to his lips. "Yer Superintendent Roy, ain't ya?" He poured half the whisky into his mouth, held it there a moment as he glared at the newcomer, and swallowed.

"Are you here at Miss Trent's request?" the newcomer enquired in a rich, warm voice laced with a strong Edinburgh accent.

"We are," Mr Skinner replied in his soft Dublin accent.

"Then I'm he," Superintendent Roy confirmed.

Mr Heath moved to a chair between his fellow Bow Streeters.

"And you're correct: I'm late," Superintendent Roy glanced at Dr Weeks. "The storm has made coach travel treacherous. Yet, I was keenly aware of you waiting here for me, so, I journeyed on foot from the harbour."

"It must be lovely to live by the sea," Mr Heath remarked.

Superintendent Roy gave a polite smile. "I reside in Edinburgh, where the Northern Lighthouse Board has its main office."

Superintendent Roy had a carefulness to his speech. It reminded Dr Weeks of his old mentor, Dr Holmwood of St. Bartholomew's Hospital in London.

"I presume you are," Superintendent Roy retrieved a letter from his jacket pocket and read its middle passage. He looked to Mr Heath. "Dr Percy Weeks," to Mr Skinner, "Mr Bertram Heath," to Dr Weeks, "And Mr Callahan Skinner?"

Dr Weeks smirked and drank the remaining whisky from his glass. "Yer ain't even close." Sitting up straight as he put his glass beside the bottle, he pointed at himself and the others. "*I'm* Dr Weeks, surgeon. *That's* Mr Skinner who's bodyguard to Captain and Lady Mirrell, and *that's* Mr Heath, an architect."

"An intriguing combination," Superintendent Roy remarked as he returned the letter to his jacket. "It's a pleasure, gentlemen." He flashed them a smile. "Rest assured, you shall be suitably compensated for the cost and inconvenience of journeying here, regardless of the outcome of your investigation."

Dr Weeks picked up his empty glass. "Ya can start by buyin' the next round."

"But of course," Superintendent Roy said. "Mr Grieves, would you be so kind?"

"Aye, Mr Roy," the innkeeper replied. He took their order and hurried to the kitchen.

"Both I and the NLB appreciate the Society's assistance and discretion in this matter," Superintendent Roy said. "Naturally, we wish to maintain the reputation of the NLB and its employees, but, more importantly, we are keen to uncover the answers which will allow us to recompense Mr Stewart's family, should that be necessary."

"Do you t'ink 'e's dead?" Mr Skinner enquired.

"Currently, we have no evidence of anything," Superintendent Roy admitted.

Mr Grieves returned and served their drinks.

"I always find it's best to start a book at the beginning," Mr Heath said, placing a hand upon the tome in his lap. "Miss Trent's letter to *me* spoke of Mr Stewart's disappearance. Granted, I haven't any *direct* experience of investigating a disappearance, *but* I *did* assist Mr Locke with finding a hidden door and—"

"Ya told Miss Trent 'e worked at the lighthouse on Lyall Island," Dr Weeks interrupted, casting a warning glance at Mr Heath.

"That is correct," Superintendent Roy said. "Alongside Primary Keeper Wallace Friseal and Assistant Keeper Coinneach McLeod, whom locals refer to as 'Connie.' Mr Stewart was—is," he frowned, "*was* an occasional keeper."

Mr Skinner took a sip of his porter. "What do they say about his disappearance?"

Superintendent Roy picked up his ale. "He was washed away from the island's main landing by a giant wave during a storm and drowned." He took a sip and, setting down the glass, dabbed at his lips and moustache with his handkerchief. "If that had occurred, his body would have been washed up in Cutcloy Harbour by now."

"It's happened before?" Dr Weeks enquired, drinking half the Scotch whisky in his glass. Fortunately, Mr Grieves had brought a fresh bottle.

"Only once," Superintendent Roy put away his handkerchief. "Five years ago, Primary Lightkeeper Mr Joel Pottersby fell from Lyall Island into the sea. His body washed up in the harbour a few days later."

"What do Misters Friseal and McLeod say now?" Dr Weeks enquired.

Superintendent Roy furrowed his brow. "I haven't returned to Lyall Island since escorting Mr Stewart's replacement a few days ago."

Dr Weeks sat back in his chair and lit a cigarette. "How did ya hear of Mr Stewart goin' missin', if yer all the way in Edinburgh?" He took a pull from the cigarette and exhaled the smoke into the open floor between them.

"The NLB received a telegram from Mr Wainwright, the captain of the *Mesopotamia*—the vessel that delivers fresh supplies to the Lyall Lighthouse—who had sent it on Mr Friseal's behalf," Superintendent Roy explained. "Naturally, I travelled to the lighthouse as soon as the weather would allow. I was accompanied by Mr Torcull Niven, Mr Stewart's replacement. Mr Friseal and Mr McLeod told me of their suspicion that Mr Stewart must have gone to the landing during a storm, only to be washed away by the sea and drowned. I took Mr Stewart's few belongings into our possession and returned to Edinburgh with the expectation Mr Stewart's body would be washed-up in the harbour. As the days passed without news, I became convinced Mr Stewart's disappearance was no mere accident. Unfortunately, without evidence of foul play, I could not act upon my conviction. For this reason, we are reluctant to involve the police."

"Did the keepers see him fall into the sea?" Mr Skinner enquired.

"They told me they hadn't," Superintendent Roy replied.

Mr Heath softly hummed. "Could Mr Stewart have hidden somewhere on the island?"

"The possibility had occurred to me, so I had the architectural plans for the lighthouse retrieved from our archive." Superintendent Roy moved a table to stand amongst them and opened the plans, prompting Mr Heath to lean forward to look closer.

"The construction of the lighthouse took advantage of the foundations of a ruined medieval fort," Superintendent Roy explained. "It is believed the fort was constructed to guard against invasions from the English. The island itself is quite close to the shore—in lighthouse terms, at least. Whilst it is possible Mr Stewart could have concealed himself within the old fort, it's unlikely due to the addition of the lighthouse rendering several of its rooms inaccessible."

Mr Heath traced the floorplans with his finger as he hummed. "Yes, I see."

"What about the rest of the island?" Mr Skinner suggested.

"Open grassland," Superintendent Roy replied. "The old fort, lighthouse, and keepers' cottage are its only structures."

Mr Heath lifted the floorplans. "Does the fort have no lower levels?"

"It does, but they have no bearing on the foundations of either the lighthouse or cottage," Superintendent Roy replied. "Therefore, they were omitted from the plans."

Mr Heath met their client's gaze. "You searched for Mr Stewart in them, I presume?"

"I and the other keepers searched every accessible inch of the lighthouse, cottage, and fort," Superintendent Roy replied. "We found no sign of Mr Stewart. Furthermore, I have discovered no evidence to support the theory of Mr Stewart concealing himself. Nor have I learned of any reason he may have to go to such lengths."

"Lightkeepin' is a hard t'ing," Mr Skinner remarked.

"You have personal experience of it?" Superintendent Roy enquired.

"No, but I have friends who do," Mr Skinner replied.

"Are they employed by us?" Superintendent Roy enquired.

"Trinity House," Mr Skinner replied. Whilst the Northern Lighthouse Board covered lighthouses in Scotland and the Isle of Man, Trinity House covered those in England and the Channel Islands. Lighthouses in Eire and Northern Ireland were covered by Irish Lights whose head office was in Dublin. "Tough, seafarin' men who say lightkeepin' work is more unforgivin' than the sea."

"It is," Superintendent Roy agreed. "They have the safety of vessels and their crews in their hands." He took a sip of ale and dabbed at his lips and beard with his handkerchief, again. "But it is not a life a man must be condemned to. He may request redeployment, or submit his resignation, at any time."

"Did Mr Stewart?" Dr Weeks enquired, exhaling more smoke.

Superintendent Roy's brows momentarily lifted. "It was the opposite in his case. He requested to be reassigned to Lyall Island only a month ago when the former occasional lightkeeper retired. He cited a desire to be closer to relatives in Cutcloy."

Mr Heath stood and leaned over the floorplans, his face an inch from the paper as he carefully moved around the table and scrutinised every room of the lighthouse and keepers' cottage. "I'd like to measure these rooms and compare their dimensions to the original plans."

"The plans must return to Edinburgh with me," Superintendent Roy revealed.

Mr Heath straightened. "They must?"

"Why?" Dr Weeks challenged.

"They are NLB property and, as such, are restricted to NLB employees only," Superintendent Roy replied.

"*Quite* understandable." Mr Heath gave a firm nod. "You will bring them to Lyall Island, then?"

Superintendent Roy gathered up the plans and slipped them back into his jacket. "Urgent matters oblige me to return to Edinburgh in the morning. Captain

Wainwright will be waiting for you aboard the *Mesopotamia* in the harbour at eight thirty, however."

Mr Heath smiled broadly. "*Good.* I shall have *ample* time to take my measurements and draw my own plans of the fort, lighthouse, and cottage once we are on the island."

"Captain Wainwright will take you there, wait at the landing, and bring you back to Cutcloy before sunset," Superintendent Roy stated. "As unfortunate as Mr Stewart's disappearance is, the light *must* be kept burning. The disruption caused by your presence must be kept to an absolute minimum." He put his business card on the table. "I shall be contactable by telegram at this address."

Mr Skinner picked up the card and read the address. It was for the main office of the Northern Lighthouse Board at 84, George Street, Edinburgh.

Dr Weeks finished his cigarette and tossed it into the fire. "I hope fer yer sake this ain't a damn waste of my time." He stood and, plucking the bottle from the table, headed for the door. "I'm goin' to bed."

II

The new day brought a new world; the storm had ceased, the clouds had dissolved, and the sky was a brilliant blue. Fortunately, there remained sufficient wind to drive the high-sailed *Mesopotamia* across the calm sea between Cutcloy Harbour and Lyall Island. The Bow Streeters had been graced with a clear view of the island from the quayside. The bulky mass dominated the horizon and caused the waves to dramatically crash against its rocks. The lighthouse, holding a silent watch over passing vessels, appeared a brilliant white in the early morning sun. Its relatively recent construction three years prior also meant its newness was in direct and stark contrast with the ancient, weather-beaten ruins of the fort which surrounded it. The combination was one Mr Heath had never seen before. Therefore, it was one he was exceedingly keen to examine further.

"The close proximity of the island to the harbour suggests it was once accessible on foot at low tide," Mr Heath mused aloud as he looked across the top of his notebook at the island they were nearing. "If that were the case, it would've made the transportation of stone for the fort *much* easier and would explain why this *particular* rock formation was chosen." He wrote some notes in pencil. "Whether attacking by boat or by land—at low tide, that is—the enemy would've been visible by the defenders on all sides." He closed his notebook. "I will test my theory once we are on the island."

"Ya do that," Dr Weeks stated, gripping the rigging as he took a swig from his hip flask. "We'll talk to the keepers." He squinted up at the lighthouse, slipping the flask into his pocket. "I ain't stayin' 'ere longer than I have to."

"I didn't know you were susceptible to cabin fever, Doctor," Mr Skinner remarked.

"Not cabin fever," Dr Weeks replied. "Too-far-from-a-bar fever."

64

Mr Skinner chuckled softly. Looking out at the open sea, he breathed in through his nose and exhaled through his mouth. The salty air tingled his nostrils as the spray caressed his face. Summoning an image of the wide, open land of the Mirrell Estate to his mind's eye, Mr Skinner could almost smell the sweet fragrances of the freshly cut grass and flowers in the meadow. Yet, as much as he enjoyed wandering those fields unimpeded, he'd never felt the same freedom as on the open sea. Out here, the horizon wasn't fenced off. Instead, countless adventures and long-lost treasures were promised beyond it. The thought of turning his back on it all over again made his soul ache.

"Hang on, gents! We're gettin' close!" Mr Wainwright warned over the din of the waves. The ship lurched to the side as he steered it into a wave. A loud thud, accompanied by a violent shake of the ship's hull, followed as it made contact with the stone landing. In a heartbeat, two of the *Mesopotamia* crew scrambled onto it whilst their fellow crewmates hauled the heavy rope up and over the side. Mr Skinner instinctively moved to help but recoiled when he remembered he'd left his false hand at the inn for fear of it going rusty from the saltwater.

No sooner had the crew secured the boat had Dr Weeks climbed ashore. Waiting for his fellow Bow Streeters to join him, he peered up at the lighthouse and ruined fort.

"That one of the keepers?!" Dr Weeks enquired, looking back at Captain Wainwright whilst pointing up at the battlements.

"I don't see anyone," Captain Wainwright replied.

Dr Weeks looked back at the battlements and frowned when he saw they were empty. "I saw someone— up there!" He pointed again.

Captain Wainwright glanced at the hip flask in Dr Weeks' pocket and exchanged a knowing glance with his second mate. Catching the insinuation in their expressions, Dr Weeks narrowed his eyes and strode over to the steep flight of stone steps that zig-zagged up the rock face to the island proper.

"The Bow Street Society, I presume?!" a deep voice boomed from the steps' summit.

Breathing heavily with a sheen of sweat covering his bright red face, Dr Weeks gripped the iron railing for dear life as he stopped at the summit and fought to catch his breath. Squinting against the low sun at their greeter, he saw he was around fifty years old with an immense black beard and unkempt hair streaked with grey. His brown eyes bore into them as he stood with his hands held in loose fists at his sides. He wore the dark coat, trousers, cap, and boots of the Northern Lighthouse Board uniform, all of which were well-maintained. As the giant of a man came closer, Dr Weeks half-expected the stone to tremble under him.

"Er, yeah, that's us," Dr Weeks replied.

The giant's hard expression remained. "You're American."

"Canadian," Dr Weeks corrected.

"Mr Callahan Skinner, sir," the Irishman greeted, offering his hand. "Retired officer with Her Majesty's Royal Navy."

The giant's expression softened. "Mr Wallace Friseal." He gave Mr Skinner's hand a firm shake. "I'm the primary lightkeeper here, and the one in charge."

"Dr Percy Weeks, surgeon, and architect, Mr Bertram Heath," Mr Skinner pointed to them in turn. "Superintendent Roy sent word of our arrival, then?"

"He did," Mr Friseal replied. "With clear orders for us to provide assistance as long as it doesn't interfere with our duties."

"What d'ya reckon happened to Mr Stewart?" Dr Weeks enquired, curious to hear if Mr Friseal's answer matched Superintendent Roy's.

Mr Friseal's lips momentarily pressed together in a slight grimace as he failed to answer straight away. When he did, his voice was an octave lower and lacked authority. "He was swept into the sea." He turned his back upon them and walked away. "Come. You have not got long."

Dr Weeks took a deep breath to brace himself for further effort and strode after their host. Mr Skinner, accustomed to strenuous exercise, hadn't even broken a sweat during their ascent. He surpassed Dr Weeks in a few strides and fell into step beside Mr Friseal. "Why would an experienced lightkeeper like Mr Stewart go to the landin' alone?"

Mr Friseal kept his gaze fixed firmly forward. "I didnae know."

As Mr Skinner allowed him to pull away, he noticed his hands were now clenched into tight fists and his arms were rigid at his sides.

As they'd seen from the harbour, the ruined fort dominated the island. Yet, there was a surprising amount of rolling, open grassland behind and to the left of it. There were no trees, however. Upon nearing the lighthouse, they found it towered considerably higher above the battlements than they'd initially thought; it made Mr Heath giddy with excitement. To the right of the tower was a white cottage with a slate tiled roof and short chimney stack. Mr Heath was perturbed by the fact the fort's outer wall had been partially demolished to allow for the cottage's construction. On further consideration, though, he realised the ruins provided an excellent barrier against the icy wind.

"I'd like to inspect the ruins, if I may?" Mr Heath enquired once he'd joined the others at the cottage door.

Mr Friseal glared at him. "What for?"

Mr Heath hesitated, utterly taken aback by the hostile tone. "Well… To eliminate the possibility Mr Stewart is still on the island."

Mr Friseal turned to face them, blocking the door as he did so. "What is this? Mr Stewart was swept into the sea. You cannae expect to find him here."

"Superintendent Roy t'inks 'e should've been washed up in the harbour by now if 'e was," Mr Skinner said.

Although Mr Friseal was scowling when he cast a glance between them, there was a worried look in his eyes. "Do what you must. I've got to get some kip as I'm tending the light tonight." He entered the cottage, leaving the door ajar for them to follow. "Mr Niven, the superintendent's guests from England are here. Mr Skinner, Mr Heath, Dr Weeks; Mr Torcull Niven, occasional lightkeeper and Mr Stewart's replacement."

Mr Niven dried his hands and shook the Bow Streeters'. In his early twenties, his complexion lacked the harsh weathering caused by a life at sea. His face was also smooth, denoting a visit to the barbers prior to starting his stint on the island. A few strands of his cinnamon-brown hair had been bleached by the sun, turning them golden brown. His deep-set hazel eyes and low brow made him appear unintentionally grumpy. Even his broad smile failed to erase the illusion. He was attired in a white shirt whose long sleeves were rolled up to his elbows, dark trousers, and heavy black boots. He spoke with a strong, Edinburgh accent, "Good mornin', sirs."

"Mr McLeod, the assistant keeper, is tending the light," Mr Friseal informed them. "Let Mr Heath explore the ruins and give the others the tour, Mr Niven." Mr Friseal's weight caused the wooden staircase to creak as he climbed it and went around a corner, out of sight. A moment later, the loud thud of the bedroom door filled the kitchen.

"I shan't be long," Mr Heath said with bright eyes and broad smile as he bounded from the cottage, his notebook at the ready.

"The kitchen," Mr Niven indicated the low-ceilinged room in which they stood. The white paint of its plastered walls had dulled to grey over the years. The bare stone floor was swept clean, and the wooden frame around the window was devoid of rot, however. An open fire burned within the chimney breast on one side of the room, whilst a table and three chairs occupied the other. A butler's sink with a hand pump was in the corner with a single counter and wall-mounted cupboard to its left. To its right was the single window overlooking the open grassland.

Mr Niven pointed upward. "Bedroom." He crossed the room and momentarily held the back of a chair. "Our fine dining area." He indicated a second doorway. "Yard with privy." He wrapped a rag around the handle of the kettle and lifted it from the stovetop. "Tea?"

"Sure t'ing," Mr Skinner replied.

Dr Weeks opened the second door and peered out into the yard. It was surrounded by a tall stone wall. He couldn't see a gate. The privy stood in the far right-hand corner. Beyond the wall was the taller one belonging to the fort. "How d'ya get to the tower from 'ere?"

"Out front," Mr Niven replied, preparing two cups of tea.

Dr Weeks closed the door to the yard. "What d'ya reckon happened to Mr Stewart?"

"I cannae say," Mr Niven replied, taking his and Mr Skinner's cups to the table.

"Why not?" Mr Skinner enquired, sitting.

"I was not here," Mr Niven replied.

"Ya'll have an opinion, though," Dr Weeks encouraged.

"Aye," Mr Niven had a mouthful of tea.

Dr Weeks sat opposite him, beside Mr Skinner. "And?"

"Mr Stewart would have known to avoid the landing in a storm," Mr Niven replied. "Mr Friseal, being the Primary, wouldnae've let him go alone either."

"And Mr McLeod?" Dr Weeks enquired.

"Would have done what Mr Friseal told him to," Mr Niven replied.

"And the fourth fella?" Dr Weeks enquired.

Mr Niven furrowed his brow as he stared at Dr Weeks. "There's no fourth man."

"Yeah, there is," Dr Weeks said. "Thirty-ish, with brown hair and big ears."

Mr Niven pushed his lower lip against his upper as he shook his head. "There's no one like that here."

Dr Weeks narrowed his eyes. "I ain't blind—drunk or otherwise. There were a fella clear as day on the battlements when we got off the boat."

"The battlements, you say?" Mr Niven enquired.

"Over there," Dr Weeks pointed in the direction of the battlements.

Mr Niven leaned upon the table with one arm and rubbed his chin with his free hand. "You must have seen the Lyall Island ghost, then, sir."

"Ain't no damn thing as ghosts," Dr Weeks dismissed.

"I thought so, too, until I heard the wailing," Mr Niven said.

"Bullshit," Dr Weeks rebuffed.

"Mr Friseal and Mr McLeod would tell you the same," Mr Niven said. "Late at night—when there's a fog or storm—an ungodly wailing is heard across the island."

Dr Weeks leaned forward, his voice assuming a hard tone. "There ain't no such thing as ghosts. Yer've spent too much time alone, is all."

Mr Niven parted his lips.

"I ain't finished," Dr Weeks warned, prompting the lightkeeper to close his mouth. "Ya wanna know what I reckon?" He glanced over his shoulder and heard Mr Friseal's snores coming from upstairs. "That it were Mr Stewart I saw on them battlements, and Mr Heath's gonna find out where 'e's been hidin'."

III

"There is absolutely *nowhere* Mr Stewart could be hiding on this island," Mr Heath announced when he returned to the cottage. He opened his notebook upon the table to reveal detailed hand-drawn plans of the fort's upper-ground, and lower-ground floor levels. "There are no actual rooms to speak of, only shells. The few spiral stone staircases which remain are narrow and built directly into the solid rock of the walls. The walls themselves being several feet thick. The rooms on the lower ground floor are, one presumes, the remains of a dungeon. Again, I found no openings or hints within the walls which would indicate a concealed room or passageway. Aside from a few loose floor tiles—I *say* tiles, it would be more accurate to describe them as thick stone slabs—and the *unfortunate* partial demolition of the outer wall, the fort is structurally sound and solidly built." He put away his notebook.

"The slabs; could a fella move 'em?" Dr Weeks enquired.

"*I* certainly could not," Mr Heath replied.

"Could a fella with more strength than an invalid move 'em?" Dr Weeks rephrased.

Mr Heath averted his gaze as he considered his answer. "No, I dare say he couldn't."

"Where did the fella I saw on the battlements come from, then?" Dr Weeks enquired.

"Search me," Mr Heath replied, taking a bag of boiled sweets from his pocket, and popping one into his mouth before offering the bag to the others. Mr Niven eagerly took a handful, Mr Skinner declined, and Dr Weeks ignored it.

"Yer *sure* there ain't *anywhere* Mr Stewart could be hidin'?" Dr Weeks pressed.

"Yes, without taking the fort apart stone-by-stone," Mr Heath replied.

"It's the ghost, sir," Mr Niven said with a grin.

71

"To Hell with the ghost," Dr Weeks growled, tossing his chair back as he strode outside. "I'm havin' a word with McLeod." Opening the door to the tower, he halted when he saw the steep, cast-iron staircase spiralling up its centre. With his earlier exhaustion from the stone steps still fresh in his mind, and joints, he was strongly averse to attempting them. Therefore, he closed the door ajar but only went as far as the foot of the stairs. Holding the railing and peering up through the empty space in the spiral's centre, he called, "Mr McLeod?!"

"Aye!" a man's broad Scottish accent shouted back.

"Dr Percy Weeks from the Bow Street Society, can I have a word with ya?!"

Mr McLeod's face appeared from the gloom as he leaned over the railing at the stairs' summit. He was in his mid-thirties and, like the others, wore the NLB's uniform. He had dishevelled dark-brown hair, wild beard, and unkempt moustache. It was impossible for Dr Weeks to determine his height from this angle, but the way his form filled the space suggested he was on the tall side. The shade of brown in his eyes was so dark, it appeared black in the limited light, giving Mr McLeod a demonic-like appearance. "I'm tendin' the light!"

"It's daytime!"

"It's got to be cleaned! What do you want me for?!"

"What d'ya reckon happened to Mr Stewart?!"

Mr McLeod's expression darkened. "He was swept out to sea!"

"Did ya see it?"

"No!"

"Then how d'ya know 'e were?!"

Mr McLeod moved out of sight. "I've no time for this! Ask Mr Friseal!"

"I have, but I wanna hear it from ya!"

Dr Weeks felt a weight drop in his stomach as he realised there was likely a clear view of the battlements from the top of the tower. Scanning the walls for windows, he muttered a curse under his breath when he found none. He had no choice; he had to climb the damn stairs. Taking a deep breath, and muttering encouragement to himself, he began his slow and laboured ascent.

Mr McLeod must've heard him as his face reappeared from the gloom. "You're not allowed up here without Mr Friseal's say!"

"I ain't gonna tell… if ya ain't," Dr Weeks panted. He stopped halfway up as his lungs felt like they were on fire. "'Sides," Dr Weeks continued his ascent, still out of breath. "We're 'ere at Superintendent Roy's request."

Mr McLeod stood at the stairs' summit, blocking his entry to the lightroom.

Dr Weeks stopped and, panting hard, turned furious eyes upon him. "Either ya move…or yer gonna find yerself makin' friends with the floor." He knew he had neither the courage nor the strength to fight him, but he hoped McLeod felt the same. Fortunately, he stepped aside, and Dr Weeks half-stumbled into the lightroom before dropping onto the window ledge.

Reassured he wasn't about to be assaulted, Mr McLeod cautiously resumed his polishing of the lamp's lens.

Dr Weeks rested his hands upon his knees and allowed his breathing to return to normal. As he waited, he looked out the window and saw an unimpeded view of the battlements. He glanced at Mr McLeod. He was certain he would've seen the figure he had. Unless he was asleep, of course. "Who was that fella on the battlements?"

"I didnae know what you're talking about." Mr McLeod moved behind the lamp.

"I saw a fella on the battlements when I got off the boat. From 'ere, ya can see the whole fort. Unless ya were asleep, ya would've seen 'im, too, so, who were 'e?"

"The only men on this island are Mr Friseal, Mr Niven, and me."

"That ain't what I asked."

Mr McLeod stepped out from behind the lamp with a scowl. "But it's the only answer you're gonna get."

Dr Weeks stood. "Were it Mr Stewart?"

"I saw *no one*," Mr McLeod firmly stated.

"Captain Wainwright's waiting," Mr Friseal said from the stairwell.

Dr Weeks and Mr McLeod simultaneously turned to look at him.

"Return to your duties, Mr McLeod," Mr Friseal ordered. "You were told not to disrupt our work, Doctor."

Dr Weeks closed the distance between them, prompting Mr Friseal to straighten to his full height. "Somethin' ain't right on this island, either one or all of ya'll are lyin' to us. Until we get to the truth, we're gonna disrupt yer work as often as we like." He pushed past Mr Friseal and descended the stairs. Stopping after a few steps, he looked up at the lightkeepers. "We'll be back first thin' in the mornin'."

As Dr Weeks left the tower, Mr Friseal glared at his uneasy colleague.

IV

The young woman's blue eyes appeared red and raw as she stared, unblinking, at the prone form lying on the damp sand at her feet. She stood with hunched shoulders and her arms tightly folded with her hands gripping her elbows. Her dark-blue woollen dress appeared as though it had been worn for several days straight. Her dark-brown overcoat and black shoes hadn't fared much better. Dirt smudged her tired face, and her light-brown hair had been scraped into a messy bun. It was clear to Dr Weeks the woman had been blindsided by grief. *Had she known all along?* He wondered.

"You're sure?" Constable Abberline enquired. He was in his early fifties with gentle green eyes and endearing smile. He was also softly spoken, something that seemed to put the woman at ease. Having been summoned from the police station at first light, he hadn't had time to shave. Therefore, light-brown stubble covered his jaw, and his short brown hair was roughly combed.

"Aye," the woman replied in a voice tense with emotion. "That's Eòghann."

Mr Stewart had been in his early thirties when he'd died. His hazel eyes, though wide open, were dull as they pointed toward the bright blue sky. His jaw was slack—a natural occurrence in death—and his weathered complexion was ice white. A chestnut-brown, bushy moustache dominated his upper lip, but his large ears were his most distinctive feature. As soon as he'd laid eyes on him, Dr Weeks knew this was the man he'd seen on the battlements the previous day.

"Thank you, Mrs McLeod," Constable Abberline said.

"Whoa, wait a minute," Dr Weeks urged, prompting the woman to look his way. "What did ya say her name was?"

"Mrs McLeod," Constable Abberline replied.

"Any relation to Mr McLeod on Lyall Island?" Dr Weeks enquired.

"He's my husband," Mrs McLeod quietly replied.

"Now, if you dinnae mind, she needs her rest," a much older woman interjected in a stern tone. Attired in a knee-length, dark-grey coat with brown ankle boots and thick, woollen socks, her dark hair was tied in a low plait. She put her arm around Mrs McLeod and guided her away from the ghastly scene. "She's expecting a wee one in a month."

Mrs McLeod simultaneously downcast her eyes and bowed her head. Allowing the older woman to lead her away, Mrs McLeod put her hands to her own stomach and, with downturned facial features, breathed in sharply through her nose. In the second before he lost sight of her face, Dr Weeks was certain he saw her clench her jaw, thereby causing the muscle in her neck to visibly tense. If he'd had to put a bet on it, he would've said she was on the verge of emotional collapse.

"Tragic business all this," Constable Abberline remarked with genuine sorrow.

"Death usually is," Dr Weeks said, returning to Mr Stewart's body.

Like the policeman, he'd been turfed out of bed at dawn. Word of there being a surgeon at the inn had spread quickly after the Bow Streeters' arrival. It was only natural, then, for him to be sent for when Mr Stewart's body had been found washed up on the sand in Cutcloy Harbour by scavengers.

"How long has he been in the water, doctor?" Constable Abberline enquired; his pencil now poised over his open notebook. The inevitable crowd of gawkers was kept at bay by Abberline's colleagues and some quayside workers.

"Since yesterday."

Constable Abberline scanned the body to find the evidence in support of the surgeon's claim. Yet, even to his experienced eye, he failed to do so. It was true Mr

Stewart's body lacked the discolouration and swelling one would expect to see on a body that had been in the water for several days but narrowing it down to yesterday was impressive. Knowing he had failed to keep abreast of scientific developments, though, he assumed he had simply missed something that was obvious to the modern-trained eye.

"I saw 'im on the battlements when I got off the boat," Dr Weeks added.

"When?" Constable Abberline enquired, taken aback.

"*Yesterday*," Dr Weeks replied, irritated by the policeman's ignorance.

"There is no need to be angry with *me*, doctor," Constable Abberline warned in a defensive tone despite his embarrassment. "You could have seen him another time."

"And ya could learn somethin' if ya paid attention," Dr Weeks retorted.

"You're strangers here," Constable Abberline warned. "You'd be wise to remember that." He moved around the body and picked up Mr Stewart's right hand by the wrist. "His knuckles are grazed, suggesting he fought before he went into the water."

Dr Weeks gripped Constable Abberline by the shoulders and drove him away from the body. "Yeah, I saw that, thanks." He glared at the policeman as he took a swift swig of brandy from his hip flask. "Ya can examine meat all ya like when yer qualified. 'Til then, keep the Hell away, d'ya hear?"

"Mornin', officer. I'm Mr Skinner, and this is Mr Heath," the Irishman introduced as he and the architect approached Constable Abberline. "We're from the Bow Street Society like Dr Weeks here."

"I hope you're better mannered," Constable Abberline warned, shaking their hands as he introduced himself.

"Impeccably so," Mr Skinner assured.

Mr Heath kept his distance from the body, his gaze upon the horizon.

"Did 'e drown?" Mr Skinner enquired.

"I ain't gonna know 'til I get 'im opened up," Dr Weeks replied. "But 'is skull's been caved in."

"I've been talkin' with the locals. They say this is where Mr Pottersby's body was found," Mr Skinner said. "The fishermen also confirmed the current that passes Lyall Island comes into the harbour at this point."

"'E ain't been swept into the sea from the landin'," Dr Weeks said. "The last storm were the night before last and *'e*," he nudged Mr Stewart's body with his foot. "Died yesterday."

"The fella you saw on the battlements?" Mr Skinner probed.

"The one and the same," Dr Weeks confirmed. "I knew those sons of bitches were lyin' to me."

Constable Abberline's face turned bright red. "*Really* now! There's no need for language like *that*!"

Dr Weeks turned his back on the blustering policeman and walked away as he lit a cigarette. "Jus' get 'im someplace cold so I can open 'im up later."

Mr Heath and Mr Skinner caught up with their fellow Bow Streeter and walked either side of him.

"As much as I agree with you, Doctor—and I do, *wholeheartedly*—I'm at a loss as to *where* on the island Mr Stewart could've *possibly* been," Mr Heath said. "I examined the *entire* fort. I—" He stopped dead in his tracks, his eyes wide. "But of *course!*" He smiled broadly and looked between the others with a mad look in his eyes. "How *utterly* foolish I have been! It all seems so *simple* now. Of *course* he hid there; where *else* could he have been *but* there? He—" He cut himself short, again, and folded his arms. Resting his elbow upon his arm, he held his closed fingers against his chin and steadily tapped his nose with his forefinger as he hummed. "Yes…that *may* put an end to my theory. Well!" He allowed his arms to drop to his sides and strode off along the beach. "There is only *one* way to find out! Gentlemen, to Lyall Island!"

V

Mr McLeod grunted and stumbled backward, landing on the damp grass between the stone steps and cottage. In a heartbeat, Mr Friseal was upon him, his large fists inflicting a barrage of punches upon the assistant lightkeeper's head and jaw. Mr Niven threw his arms around Mr Friseal's waist and fought in vain to drag him from their colleague.

"There'll be none of that!" Constable Abberline yelled as he ran toward the trio. Despite the Bow Streeters' swift departure from the beach, the policeman had managed to intercept them at the quayside. When he'd learned of their intention to return to Lyall Island, he'd insisted upon accompanying them. Unexpectedly, Dr Weeks had welcomed the suggestion. "I said 'there'll be none of that,' Wallace Friseal!"

Mr Friseal tugged his arm free of the policeman's grip. "Away with you, George!"

Mr Niven released Mr Friseal's waist as Mr Skinner and Constable Abberline hooked their arms beneath Mr Friseal's and dragged him off Mr McLeod.

"He put an end to Eòghann!" Mr Friseal shouted, struggling against them.

"I didnae!" Mr McLeod denied, scrambling to his feet.

"He's *lying*!" Mr Friseal attempted to lunge for Mr McLeod but was forced to his knees by Mr Skinner giving their backs a swift kick. The moment he was on the ground, Constable Abberline secured the wild man's wrists behind his back with some handcuffs. When Mr Friseal then tried to stand, Constable Abberline and Mr Skinner pushed him back down by his shoulders.

"What have you got to say for yourself, Connie?" Constable Abberline demanded.

Mr McLeod paced. "I didnae murder anyone. I'll swear it on the bible if I must."

80

"It would *burn* your flesh, the *Devil* that you are!" Mr Friseal yelled.

"We don't know if Eòghann drowned or not until Dr Weeks does the post-mortem," Constable Abberline pointed out. "It could've just as easily been an accident."

"It weren't no accident!" Mr Friseal snarled.

"You don't know that, Wallace," Constable Abberline rebuffed.

"'E does," Dr Weeks said, drawing everyone's attention. He stood between Mr Friseal and Mr McLeod to address them at the same time. "Ya knew Mr Stewart were still on the island, 'cause it were impossible for ya'll *not* to see 'im on the battlements when ya'll were tendin' the light." Addressing Mr Friseal, he continued, "Yer in charge of this island, and ya ain't the kinda man to let things go to wreck and ruin. I also reckon ya knew Mr Stewart were still on the island 'cause ya helped 'im hide in the first place." Addressing Mr McLeod, he said, "They wanted ya to see 'im on the battlements." He then enquired from Mr Friseal, "Didn't ya?"

"*Aye*," Mr Friseal replied through gritted teeth. Yet, for all he was glaring at Dr Weeks, the murderous rage had disappeared from his eyes. "We wanted this blaggard to know the truth was out." He indicated Mr McLeod with a movement of his head.

"What truth?" Mr Heath enquired, enthralled by the conversation.

Mr Friseal and Mr McLeod glared at each other but neither spoke.

"Mrs McLeod losin' her baby," Dr Weeks replied, regaining their attention.

Mr McLeod's glare intensified. "What if she did? That's no business of yours."

"You put an end to that poor, wee bain, and Eòghann knew it!" Mr Friseal yelled.

"It was her own stupid fault; she fell down the stairs," Mr McLeod angrily rebuffed.

Mr Friseal attempted to lunge at him but was forced back to his knees by Constable Abberline and Mr Skinner's weight upon his shoulders. "You almost *murdered* the poor lass!"

"How did *you* know?" Mr Heath enquired from Dr Weeks.

"Workin' with the dead, ya see a lot of grievin' folk. She had eyes which looked like they'd been cryin' fer weeks," Dr Weeks explained. "Eòghann were found this mornin'. She were numb when she saw his body. It weren't 'til her friend said 'bout her baby that she looked like she were 'bout to become hysterical."

"Superintendent Roy told us he had searched the lighthouse, cottage, fort, and island, though," Mr Heath pointed out, his mind awhirl with questions.

"To be sure their deception wasn't discovered, Mr Friseal told Captain Wainwright to report Mr Stewart's 'fate' to Superintendent Roy," Mr Skinner thought aloud, the pieces of the puzzle falling into place in his mind. "A man swept out to sea is tragic but not uncommon in lightkeepin'." He recalled his friends' stories from their time working for Trinity House. Then there was Mr Pottersby's accident. "I t'ink Mr McLeod went along with the lie because it was his superior telling it. You probably hadn't thought Superintendent Roy would be investigatin' it, Mr Friseal—"

"I knew he would," Mr Friseal interrupted. "That's why *we*," he glanced at Mr McLeod, "had to agree Eòghann was swept out to sea. I led the search—but made sure the superintendent thought he had—and kept them away from Eòghann's hiding place."

"And, with folks thinkin' 'e were dead, Mr Stewart could confront Mr McLeod without consequence," Dr Weeks said in a harsh tone. "No questions asked."

"Aye," Mr Friseal admitted. "Only *he* took it too far." He glared at Mr McLeod.

"I didnae mean to hurt him," Mr McLeod insisted.

"Like you didnae mean to hurt your wife and bain?!" Mr Friseal demanded.

"She *fell*!" Mr McLeod shouted.

"I didnae believe a word you say!" Mr Friseal yelled.

"Why don't you tell us what happened with Mr Stewart, Connie?" Constable Abberline invited.

Mr McLeod felt his anger wane at the policeman's respectful tone, and, so, he explained, "Eòghann had been hiding on the island since he had 'gone into the sea.' I saw him on the battlements and, aye, he wanted me to see him." He shifted his gaze to Dr Weeks, "After you left, I saw him again. Only this time, I followed him to his hiding place. He was as wild as he is," he gestured to Mr Friseal, "accusing me of murdering my wee unborn bain. I tried telling him it was an accident, that she fell down the stairs, but he was not having any of it. He pushed me, so I pushed him back. He must have been close to the edge because he was gone in the blink of an eye."

"You *murdered* the poor lad!" Mr Friseal snarled.

"That's *enough*!" Constable Abberline ordered. "Mr Niven, please lock Mr McLeod in the tower. Mr Friseal, you'll be put into the cottage. I'll take you *both* to Cutcloy once we're done here." Pulling Mr Friseal to his feet with Mr Skinner's assistance, the policeman felt no resistance from the much taller man. In fact, the primary and assistant lightkeepers permitted the others to lead them away without incident.

"I'll need someone to take their place," Mr Niven remarked once he had regrouped with the policeman and Bow Streeters outside the cottage.

"We'll send a telegram to Superintendent Roy in Edinburgh," Mr Skinner said.

Mr Niven muttered a quiet, "thank you." Nevertheless, he remained daunted by the idea of manning the lighthouse alone until replacements arrived.

"Where was Mr Stewart hiding?" Constable Abberline enquired from the Bow Streeters.

"I believe *I* know," Mr Heath announced in triumph.

"You said there was nowhere before," Mr Niven pointed out.

"One cannot be correct all the time," Mr Heath muttered, feeling his face warm. "*But* if you would care to follow me, gentlemen, I shall show you."

Constable Abberline followed the architect as he strode off toward the ruins with Mr Niven and Mr Skinner close behind. Loitering to take a swift swig from his hip flask, Dr Weeks then caught up with them by the fort's partially demolished wall. Climbing through after them, he shivered as the wind swirled around the space, chilling his core. He'd grown up in Canada—one of the coldest places in the civilised world—but this wasn't cold; this was like standing in an ice store wearing nothing more than what you were born with. Pulling his coat tightly around himself, he folded his arms and went across the shell of a room after the others and descended a stone spiral staircase into a dark underground room.

"It's darker than a night on the Atlantic," Mr Skinner observed.

"Is it?" Mr Heath enquired. "Yes, I suppose it is. It shouldn't be too bad once your eyes have adjusted."

"I ain't waitin' that long. Abberline, ya got a truncheon?" Dr Weeks enquired.

"Certainly," Constable Abberline replied.

"Can I borrow it?" Dr Weeks enquired, irritated by the policeman's slowness.

Constable Abberline fumbled in the dark and gave it to him. "It's police property. Please, don't damage it."

"The Society'll buy ya a new one," Dr Weeks said.

A few moments later, the others heard the striking of a match. This was swiftly followed by Dr Weeks' face being illuminated as the brandy-soaked scarf he'd wrapped around the truncheon ignited to create a makeshift torch.

"How ingenious," Mr Heath complimented.

"Deadly, too, if what yer've got to show us ain't worth sacrificin' my brandy for," Dr Weeks warned.

Mr Heath gave a feeble smile but knew the surgeon was serious. "Quite." He led them to the far corner of the room where he crouched and slipped his fingers beneath the corner of a large, stone slab. "As I told you yesterday, gentlemen, I found these slabs were loose during my inspection. They were far too heavy for me to lift, and so I *presumed* any other man would find it just as impossible, but one must always *test* a theory." He gave a loud grunt as he tried to lift the slab.

Releasing it a moment later, he dug his fingers deeper into the gap between the two slabs and, holding his breath, tried to lift it again with every ounce of his strength. His face swiftly turned bright red from the exertion but, finally, he succeeded in lifting and sliding the slab away. Falling backwards, he threw out his hands to catch himself. Breathless, he dabbed at his face with his handkerchief. "Please, look for yourselves, gentlemen."

Dr Weeks held the torch over the space the slab had previously occupied and saw a set of stone steps leading downward. He exchanged surprised glances with the others but made no move to descend.

"After you," Mr Skinner invited.

"I ain't goin' down there," Dr Weeks scoffed.

"He's right; we don't know what we might find," Constable Abberline agreed.

"I'll go." Mr Skinner took the torch and wedged it between his iron fingers. Drawing his revolver with his natural hand, he descended the steps with both items held close to his body. "If everyone's tellin' the truth, I'll find no one down here."

"But the ghost," Mr Niven remarked.

"Ya'll become a ghost if ya don't quit spoutin' that bullshit," Dr Weeks warned.

Meanwhile, Mr Skinner put his back to a wall at the foot of the stairs and peered around the corner. A moment later, he moved out of sight.

"What've yer found?!" Dr Weeks yelled.

"See for yourself!" Mr Skinner replied.

Dr Weeks moved back from the hole to allow the others to go ahead of him. There was a reason why he'd stayed in the surgeon's tent instead of the battlefield when he was enlisted by the British back in Canada.

Finding himself in near pitch blackness once he'd reached the foot of the stairs, he found the wall and felt along it until he came to the corner. Shuffling around it, he halted when he caught daylight out the corner of his eye. Turning fully, he saw it was coming from a partially submerged cave mouth on the opposite side of an underground body of water.

"It's almost identical to the landing we disembarked at," Mr Heath observed. "Undoubtedly built as an escape route for the fort's occupants should it fall into enemy hands."

"It's definitely where Mr Stewart's been livin' for the past few weeks," Mr Skinner said as he held the torch over a blanket, unlit lantern, and some remnants of food strewn across the far end of the landing.

"Yeah." Dr Weeks crouched beside the landing's edge and, lighting a match, held the flame over the murky water. Seeing large, jagged rocks protruding from its depths, he softly added, "And where 'e died."

VI

Miss Trent put down Dr Weeks' report and rested her clasped hands upon it as she looked across at him. They sat in the meeting room at Bow Street—she at its head and him at its foot. The fire snapped and crackled in the hearth, and the gas lamps burned with a small flame. It was coming up to nine forty-five at night, but their discussion had only begun an hour previous.

She'd been informed that Mr Skinner and Mr Heath had returned to their respective homes as soon as the trio had returned to London, which was understandable given the hour. Dr Weeks had been subdued since his arrival; a thing so unheard of, she half-suspected she was dreaming. Her dark-brown eyes took in his body language; he sat sideways, facing the wall, with his foot on the chair diagonal to his own and the knee of the same leg bent. His wrist rested on the knee, allowing his hand to hang loose over the top of his shin. His other elbow rested upon the table, and he was slouched in the chair with his shoulders just above the backrest. He was staring into the distance with a sombre expression and glazed-over eyes.

"A tragic case," Miss Trent observed in a sympathetic voice.

"Yeah," Dr Weeks quietly agreed as his eyes became downcast.

Miss Trent moved her chair in front of his and sat.

She was attired in a dark-red, cotton bustle dress with long sleeves and high neckline to ward off the cold. Her chestnut-brown corkscrew ringlets cascaded down the back of her head and neck like a waterfall. At twenty-eight, she was younger than him by a year.

"Do you want to talk about it?" she invited in a gentle tone.

"I have." Dr Weeks kept his gaze on his knee as he lit a cigarette. "Roy ain't gonna be happy, but we did what 'e asked; we found Stewart." He took a deep pull from the cigarette and, closing his eyes, momentarily leaned his back whilst exhaling the smoke. The sensation of her hand upon his knee caused his gaze to dart to her, however. A sense of shared sorrow passed between them before Dr Weeks pulled his knee away and put his foot on the floor. "There ain't anythin' to talk 'bout. A fella's dead, so's 'is unborn niece or nephew, and the one responsible is gonna walk free. That's all there is to it."

"You stated in your report that you couldn't be certain either way about Mr McLeod's culpability."

"Scientifically speakin', yeah, but any damn fool can see 'e's guilty as sin."

"We aren't the police."

Dr Weeks stood, a fierce scowl upon his face. "Nah, we ain't." He strode over to the fireplace but turned sharply and returned just as swiftly. "But *that's* the *damn* problem! We *know* the sonofabitch is guilty, but there ain't a *thing* we can do about it!"

"That isn't true."

"I don't reckon the local coppers'll look kindly on us stringin' 'im up," Dr Weeks sardonically rebuffed.

Miss Trent stood. "You *know* that isn't what I meant, Weeks."

Dr Weeks leaned into her personal space. "I don't see anythin' else that can be done."

Maintaining her ground, she had a defiant look in her eyes as she challenged him with a subtle lift of her chin. "Firstly, I will give our findings to Superintendent Roy alongside the Society's recommendations that, one, Mr McLeod is removed from the service of the Northern Lighthouse Board and, two, Mr Friseal is permitted to return to Lyall Island as primary lightkeeper. Secondly, I will offer Mrs McLeod the sanctuary of this house by communicating with her through Constable Abberline. Thirdly, if she declines, I will request Constable Abberline to keep me abreast of her situation in the form of weekly letters. If, at any time, I fear she may be in danger from her husband, I have Mr Skinner's permission to send him to Cutcloy to intervene on the Society's behalf."

Dr Weeks continued to glare at her. The tension in his face then slowly eased, and the corners of his mouth lifted into a smile. With a brief shake of his head, he complimented, "Yer something' else, d'ya know that?"

Miss Trent smiled. "I wouldn't be the clerk of the Bow Street Society if I wasn't."

Dr Weeks chuckled.

VII

It was several weeks later and Mr Niven's turn to do the nightshift. The white of the full moon was made more intense by the pitch blackness of the cloudless sky and calm sea. Sitting on a hardbacked wooden chair before the front facing windows, Mr Niven read *Treasure Island* by Robert Louis Stevenson. He had just reached the part where Billy Bones dies of a heart attack when a horrific wail cut through the night, causing him to leap from his chair, tossing his book in the process. With his own heart pounding, and his breathing becoming shallow yet laboured, Mr Niven crept up to the window and peered through the glass.

There, on the battlements, was Mr Pottersby and Mr Stewart looking back at him.

Mr Niven gasped and dropped to the floor.

The wailing resumed.

Mr Niven covered his ears but could still hear it.

The wailing continued, but Mr Niven soon realised it was getting quieter as the moments passed. Trembling from head to toe, he slowly peered over the window ledge.

Mr Pottersby and Mr Stewart had their backs turned and, as they walked across the black abyss of the ruined fort, the wailing grew quieter, still.

Mr Niven watched, unable to breathe or even blink.

The two lightkeepers faded as the wailing died away.

Mr Niven released a loud sigh and dropped back to the floor.

Peace had returned to Lyall Island.

The Case of the Bold Blackmailer

I

Sitting at the table in the Society's kitchen, Miss Dexter planned to draw Miss Trent as she rolled out some pastry for a batch of mince pies. Unfortunately, the more she stared at the blank page, the more her mind was filled with the events of a few days ago. She still couldn't believe it; it was so horrible, and yet, so tragic. Neither Maxwell had deserved what had befallen them. She felt her heart ache.

Attired in midnight-blue bustle skirts and blouse, the eighteen-year-old artist's auburn hair was neatly wrapped in a bun at the base of her skull and adorned with plain silver pins. They, and the silver brooch pinned to the collar of her blouse, sparkled in the lamplight.

A full decade older than her friend, Miss Trent was also three inches taller at five foot seven. Her attire consisted of plum bustle skirts with a lilac panel at their front, a plum jacket with silk lapels, a cream blouse with ruffled detailing, and a broad, black belt with brass buckle. An apron was also tied around her waist. Like Miss Dexter's, the gold and ivory brooch pinned to her blouse's high neck occasionally caught the lamp's light. Finally, aside from a few loose curls against her back, her chestnut-brown hair was pinned atop her head in an elaborately sculpted mass.

Setting aside her rolling pin, Miss Trent looked to Miss Dexter with the intention of enquiring after the progress of her sketch. The sight of the artist's green eyes staring, unblinkingly, through the page at something unseen beneath made her frown, however. It had been hard on them all, but Miss Dexter had taken it to heart.

"Red shirt's in the livery," Mr Snyder's rough, East End of London-accented voice remarked from the doorway. With a calloused and cracked thumb pointing over his shoulder, his brown, beady eyes looked between his friends. Broad in build, his black bushy sideburns and short hair appeared more unkempt than usual. His brown jacket, dark-brown trousers, and worn, black leather boots were also damp in places. At forty-eight, he was the most senior in the group.

"Is it still snowing?" Miss Trent enquired.

"Yeah but not as heavy," Mr Snyder replied, taking a seat opposite Miss Dexter.

"Good." Miss Trent carefully cut circles out of the pastry and scooped a spoonful of filling into the centre of each. "Am I moving too much?"

"Hmm?" Miss Dexter lifted her head. Realising what she'd said, she offered a polite smile. "Not at all." With a melancholic expression, she set down her sketchbook and pencil. "I haven't been able to draw anything."

"Inspiration will come, lass," Mr Snyder gently encouraged.

Miss Trent cut out smaller circles from her pastry and, placing them upon her filling, carefully pinched the two edges to form a seal. Putting them in the oven to cook, she wiped her hands upon her apron and put some tea things upon the table.

"The water should be boiled now," Miss Trent said as the sound of knocking took her from the room. Removing her apron as she did, she placed it upon the side table as she crossed the hallway.

"Is *this* the Bow Street Society?" demanded the woman revealed to be standing upon the porch when Miss Trent opened the door. She was attired in a red bustle dress, dark-red waist-length jacket, and tall, black hat adorned with red fabric flowers and berries, and black ribbon. In her mid-forties, she had chocolate-brown hair tied up in an elaborately coiled bun upon her crown. The hat perched upon the front of her head, its brim jutting out above her eyes and partially covering her forehead.

"It is, I'm—" Miss Trent began.

"I shall expect the Society's representatives at my residence in Buckinghamshire at one o'clock tomorrow afternoon," the woman interrupted, thrusting a small envelope toward Miss Trent. "My address."

Miss Trent kept her gaze fixed upon the woman.

A moment of inactivity passed.

The woman's facial muscles tightened as she did a half-roll of her eyes. "I am more than capable of paying whatever fee the Society demands."

"Except the humble fee of *politeness*," Miss Trent retorted and began to close the door. "Good day."

"I have travelled all the way from Wolverton on a foul-smelling, ill-upholstered steam train to come here," the woman said, raising her voice a fraction and thereby compelling Miss Trent to keep the door open. "I *demand* to be heard."

Miss Trent considered dismissing the woman anyway. Deciding it was better to act in the charitable spirit of Christmas than risk causing a scene in full view of the street, though, she stepped aside. "Please, come in."

The woman looked from Miss Trent to the doorway's threshold and back again. "I have given my address and shall give the particulars of my case to your representatives tomorrow. There is nothing further to say."

Miss Trent placed a hand upon her hip. "As clerk of the Bow Street Society it is *me* you give the particulars to, *not* its members."

"But—"

"It isn't a matter for debate," Miss Trent pointedly interrupted.

The woman released a loud sigh and strode inside. "I shall tell you what it is; it is *incorrigible*!"

Miss Trent gave a defiant lift of her chin. "The only one being incorrigible is you, Mrs…?"

"*Gove*," the woman replied.

"Everythin' okay?" Mr Snyder enquired from the kitchen doorway with Miss Dexter standing behind him, peering over his shoulder.

"Yes, thank you, Sam," Miss Trent replied. To the visitor, she said, "This is Mr Snyder and Miss Dexter, members of the Bow Street Society." Her gaze shifted back to them. "Mrs Gove is here to ask for the Society's help. Miss Dexter, could you bring us some tea in the parlour and take my pies from the oven?"

"Of course," Miss Dexter replied with a small nod.

"Thank you," Miss Trent said.

As she indicated the open doorway, Miss Dexter and Mr Snyder returned to the kitchen.

II

Mrs Gove's eyes were devoid of emotion as she viewed the parlour's fir tree. A string of small, brass bells was wrapped loosely around its branches, and crude clay baubles acted as counterweights to the slender, white candles fixed to its branches. Mrs Gove lifted the string of bells with one finger and inspected them. Releasing them, she muttered, "How tawdry."

Miss Trent cast a critical eye over Mrs Gove's attire and quietly stated, "I agree."

"Do you often slap the hand that pays you?" Mrs Gove enquired as she crossed the room and plucked the Virgin Mary from the hand-carved Nativity scene on the mantelshelf.

"You haven't paid me anything, aside insults."

"My request was a perfectly reasonable one," Mrs Gove returned the Virgin Mary to the scene. "The Society should make its expectations clear in its advertisements for clients."

Miss Trent visualised the wording to which Mrs Gove referred and concluded it was sufficient in its clarity. Deciding to navigate away from the topic, she indicated the sofa and invited Mrs Gove to sit whilst she took the armchair. A moment later, Miss Dexter entered with the tea tray and set it down on the table before the fire. Miss Trent gave her an appreciative smile, "Thank you."

"Is she an orphan?" Mrs Gove enquired following Miss Dexter's departure.

"Not at all." Miss Trent poured the tea.

"She has a melancholy about her that suggests she is," Mrs Gove accepted her cup and added cream and sugar. "Orphans have my sympathy."

The few who do, Miss Trent thought as she sipped her tea.

"Exemplary," Mrs Gove complimented after her first taste. Taking a second, she set the cup and saucer down upon the table. "May I rely upon the discretion of you and the Bow Street Society, Miss Trent?"

"Yes, unless a crime has been committed."

"Not by me." Mrs Gove glanced over her shoulder. "But Mrs *Ignatius* Bloomingdale."

Miss Trent retrieved her notebook and pencil from the mantelshelf to record the conversation in shorthand. "What is her crime?"

"Blackmail."

"Of whom?"

"*Me*," Mrs Gove replied in a raised voice as spots of colour entered her cheeks. "It *must* be stopped." She picked up her tea and lifted the cup from its saucer. "She denies it." She brought the cup to her lips but immediately replaced it upon the saucer. "And no evidence exists because her demands are given when we are alone." She returned the cup and saucer to the table. "If that *silly* girl had not written her *accursed* letter—!" She held clasped hands to her mouth and exhaled loudly through her nose. Momentarily closing her eyes, she returned her hands to her lap. "It has been a very trying time."

Miss Trent offered Mrs Gove's tea back to her. "I understand."

"Thank you." Mrs Gove drained the cup, leading Miss Trent to suspect her drink of choice at home was something considerably stronger. "Mrs Bloomingdale employs a former governess of ours, Miss Stephanie Lauder. It was *she* who penned the letter—the grounds on which Mrs Bloomingdale blackmails me. I shall pay any price to have it in my hands."

Miss Trent halted in her notetaking to scrutinise Mrs Gove. "We shan't." She set down her pencil and lifted her head. "The Bow Street Society isn't a means through which you may break the law, regardless of the reasons. We may speak to Mrs Bloomingdale on your behalf—even act as mediators to purchase the letter—but that is as far as I'm willing to allow our members to go, Mrs Gove."

"There are plenty at the public house who would abandon their scruples for money," Mrs Gove sneered. "That is not my proposal, Miss Trent."

"As long as we understand one another."

Mrs Gove's cheeks tightened. "We do."

Miss Trent picked up her pencil. "What does the letter contain?"

"I'd rather not say," Mrs Gove replied in a quiet voice. "Is it imperative you know?"

Miss Trent considered the question. "No." She looked Mrs Gove full in the face. "Provided you give your solemn word it isn't criminal in nature."

Mrs Gove gave a curt nod of her head. "You have it."

"May I ask how much money Mrs Bloomingdale has extorted from you?"

"None whatsoever."

Miss Trent lowered her pencil. "Then how—?"

"She has threatened to publicly reveal the letter's contents if I do not attend her *awful* afternoon teas and *dull* dinner parties. She is extorting my *time* from me, Miss Trent and, with it, my respectable reputation."

"I see." Miss Trent understood what her client was saying, but nonetheless marvelled at how simplistic and comfortable these women's lives must be if social gatherings, and who attended them, were their only concerns.

Mrs Gove stood suddenly, her elbows held rigidly against her sides. Her hands were clasped so tightly against her stomach, they lost their colour. "May I expect the Bow Street Society tomorrow?"

Miss Trent set aside her notebook and pencil. "You may."

"I shall see myself out."

Miss Trent watched her hurried departure and, upon hearing the front door close, softly muttered, "Wonders never cease."

III

The snow-covered countryside moved past the first-class compartment's window. Sitting to the left of it, facing inward, was freelance journalist of the *Truth* and *Women's Signal* publications, Lady Katheryne Owston. Sitting opposite was her secretary and ward, Miss Agnes Webster. They gently rocked with the train's movement as they mulled over their latest Bow Street Society assignment.

In her early twenties, Miss Webster had chocolate-brown hair scraped into a bun at the base of her skull. Attired in a cotton bustle dress of muted browns and reds, she'd made sure to be as uninteresting in her appearance as possible. Catching the eyes of men had never been one of her ambitions as marriage was a spirit-draining existence she'd intentionally avoided. Her cheeks were pink from the cold, whilst her hazel eyes were glazed over with boredom. The recent events surrounding Mr Maxwell and the Bow Street Society had been emotionally intense, but also exciting in a bizarre way. It was unsurprising, then, that she was reluctant to travel to a town she'd neither heard of nor visited, albeit on Society business. *Wolverton,* she thought. *Were wolves bred there in days gone by? Or is it so named because the nature of its people is as beastly as its name?* She conceded the latter was merely a cruel and unfair assumption, but the town's unusual name called for further scrutiny, nonetheless.

A few wrinkles in the corners of Lady Owston's eyes denoted her forty-seven years. Yet the fashionable style she'd put her warm, chestnut-brown hair was evidence she'd avoided the trap of drabness women her age seemed to inevitably fall into. *One must not try to look older than one's years,* was her motto. *One will be old soon enough; there is no need to hasten the process.* Attired in a vibrant teal, cotton bustle dress, she'd made sure it was as elaborately decorated as possible with beads, lace, and silk. An ankle-length, brown fur coat protected her from the cold. She folded Miss Trent's note and returned it to its envelope as she announced, "Mrs Gove resides on Cambridge Street and Mrs Bloomingdale on Windsor Street."

The sound of movement in the corridor drew her gaze to the passing conductor. Briefly lifting her hand to acknowledge the tipping of his hat, she smiled politely at him until he was out of sight. The gleam in his eyes was suggestive of the zeal with which he'd procured a porter when she had enquired after the Wolverton train at Euston railway station. Their disappointment had been palatable when Miss Webster had revealed they had no luggage. Lady Owston had assumed they'd genuinely wanted to assist them, whereas Miss Webster had assumed they'd genuinely wanted the tip.

"According to Mr Snyder, Wolverton Works manufactures railway carriages, including the *royal train* for Her Majesty," Lady Owston continued with delight. "He also explained that, given its location, Wolverton is a convenient place to change locomotives and replenish the train's supplies."

"Did he say Her Majesty was due to visit?" Miss Webster enquired in her usual monotone.

"He did not know, but no one would, dear. As one would expect, Her Majesty's schedule is a closely guarded secret."

"A pity," Miss Webster sighed. "It would've made our stay considerably more interesting."

"Now, now, Agnes." Lady Owston wagged her finger. "We cannot be solving gruesome murders every day." She added under her breath, "Thankfully."

Miss Webster kept her thoughts to herself.

"The *London and Birmingham Railway Company* own both the works *and* the railway station," Lady Owston continued. "Mr Snyder explained there would be a station master on hand to direct us to Cambridge Street."

Miss Webster hummed. "We are not staying overnight, are we?"

"No; I rather expect we shall have this matter resolved by dinner time."

"An expectation I share—wholeheartedly."

"*Really*, Agnes, you speak as though Wolverton were in the middle of nowhere instead of a short train ride from London," Lady Owston scolded.

"And yet it seems London's liveliness has failed to reach it," Miss Webster observed as the train passed rows of uniform red-brick warehouses with slanted roofs.

The buildings, surrounding walls, and ground had a covering of grey-looking snow. *Soot and mud*, Miss Webster inwardly observed. *It looks more mugshot than picture postcard.* The station the train pulled into hadn't fared much better: a thick layer of snow covered the roofs of the platforms' covered staircases, whilst dark-grey slush had been swept into piles against their wooden walls. The station was a large house-like structure with a tiled roof at the top of a hill. A high, red-brick wall that ran off to the right of it denoted the bridge that allowed pedestrians and traffic to pass over the railway lines and into Wolverton proper.

Miss Webster pulled the window down and, reaching outside, lifted the external handle as the train slowed to a stop. Alighting first, she used her hand to shield her eyes from the low hanging sun as she peered down the platform through the dissipating steam. Despite being a direct line to London, there were only a handful of passengers who disembarked. There were no signs of any porters, either. Spying a covered stairwell at the opposite end of the platform once the steam had cleared, Miss Webster turned to her guardian as she joined her. Slamming shut their compartment's door, she slipped her hand into the crook of Lady Owston's elbow and walked with her toward the stairwell.

A middle-aged man in a dark-blue coat, trousers, tie, and hat came down the stairs at the same time. His fair yet rugged complexion and a light-brown moustache and whiskers gave him a weathered but dignified appearance.

The spotless surface of his cap's black peek mimicked the shine of his black leather boots, the silver pocket watch chain across his waistcoat, and the brass whistle in his hand. His blue eyes were welcoming as they looked to Lady Owston and Miss Webster, and he swiftly acknowledged their presence with a brief touch of his cap's peek. "Good afternoon, ladies," he greeted upon approaching them.

"Good afternoon," Lady Owston said, halting to speak with him. When he walked past them, though, she turned to follow him with her gaze and watched as he made his checks and sent the train on its way with a shrill peal of his whistle.

Miss Webster was impressed by his efficiency.

Lady Owston shifted her weight from one foot to the other to keep warm and tucked her gloved hands into her coat's sleeves as she tutted softly, her eyes fixed upon the man's doings.

"May I be of assistance, ladies?" the man enquired upon noticing they remained.

"You may," Lady Owston replied, striding over to him. "*I* am Lady Katheryne Owston, and *this* is my secretary and ward, Miss Agnes Webster. *We* have come from *London*, sir, and it is our first visit to Wolverton. I am *certain* you would want us to tell our friends of the *impeccable* hospitality we received here, *especially* from the station master."

"I'm he," the man said. "Mr Harold Ravendale." He offered a friendly smile. "I'm pleased to meet you both."

"And we you," Lady Owston said.

"How may I be of assistance?" Mr Ravendale enquired.

"We are visiting a friend who resides on Cambridge Street," Lady Owston replied. "Could you provide us with some directions, please?"

Mr Ravendale's eyes twinkled. "You could walk, or you could take the Wolverton to Stony Stratford

101

Tramway." He pointed to the bridge upon which the station house stood. "The tram should be there any minute. It's late because it probably had to be pushed up the hill on account of the snow. You can take it to the Print Works and walk along Stratford Road until you get to the junction with Cambridge Street."

"*Thank* you, sir," Lady Owston said with a broad smile. "*Come*, Agnes!"

Miss Webster gave Mr Ravendale an emotionless glance as she followed her guardian who had already stridden a fair distance away.

The station house's floor was unvarnished boards covered in scratches, whilst the interior walls were painted white. The latter had become dull over the years, becoming a subtle shade of grey. Upon stepping into the main ticket hall, Lady Owston and Miss Webster saw the window for the ticket office was on the left. Opposite was the parcel office. A set of double doors directly opposite the stairs led to the street. Finally, two further covered flights of stairs and a goods lift led to the remaining platform. Considering the number of platforms, the station was quieter than one would expect.

Neither Lady Owston nor Miss Webster had any trouble finding the tram stop since a small steam locomotive was slowing to a stop beside it. Attached to the locomotive's rear was a narrow yet tall carriage. Both were on iron rails embedded into the ground.

Climbing aboard, the Bow Streeters took the seats on the second row, and Miss Webster paid for their tickets with the ticket conductor as the tram trundled forward. Over the course of their brief journey, he explained the tram was timed to coincide with the arrival of the trains during the day, but its main function was to bring the workers to and from Wolverton and Stony Stratford in the mornings and evenings. He also sheepishly confirmed Mr Ravendale's suspicion about the tram needing to be pushed up the snow-covered hill. Miss Webster glanced around at the near-deserted tram and found herself conceding it was a more pleasant experience than the crowded ones in London. *This may not be such an unpleasant visit after all*, she inwardly mused.

IV

In her early forties, Mrs Ignatius Bloomingdale had what Lady Owston could only describe as an unremarkable face. Her nose, cheekbones, and jaw were fine enough in isolation but, as a collective, they failed to strike a chord. Mrs Bloomingdale's dark-blue eyes did her a further disservice as their half-moon shape gave the illusion of fatigue. Even her blond hair, although impeccably arranged in a fashionably coiled plait, had a dullness to its colour. Her only saving grace was her fitted dark-blue jacket over a cream, frilled blouse, and straight-lined, dark-blue skirts.

The Bow Streeters' visit to Mrs Gove at home had been a brief one. She'd repeated her story to them and, again, refused to divulge the contents of the offensive letter in Mrs Bloomingdale's possession. Conceding they couldn't break her silence and keen to return to London before nightfall, they'd walked the short distance to Mrs Bloomingdale's house.

"As delighted as I am to have you in my home, I fail to see how I may be of assistance to a freelance fashion journalist and her secretary," Mrs Bloomingdale said as she passed Lady Owston's calling card back to her. The Bow Streeters sat on the sofa whilst Mrs Bloomingdale occupied a low-backed armchair. Directly opposite the sofa was the fire within the parlour's hearth.

The heels of Miss Webster's gloved hands rested in her lap as she repeatedly flexed her intertwined fingers. Her gaze moved between her hands and Mrs Bloomingdale, lingering on one for a moment before returning to the other. She'd closed her eyes during the transition, though, to avoid seeing the fire. Nevertheless, she felt her face warm, her breathing shallow, and her throat tighten. Convinced she was on the verge of being overcome by fear, she stood and crossed to the window. Alas, there was no draft to speak of, despite the rot of the frame.

"Is there something the matter?" Mrs Bloomingdale enquired with ghoulish curiosity.

"No," Miss Webster replied in a wavering voice. She downcast her gaze as she turned to their host and said in a subdued voice, "I need some air. Excuse me."

Mrs Bloomingdale rose to follow her as she hurried from the room, but Lady Owston's voice stayed her. "I'll go. Excuse me, please."

"I'm fine," Miss Webster dismissed the moment Lady Owston joined her in the front garden. "I'll join you, again, in a few moments."

Lady Owston furrowed her brow as she watched her ward with deep concern. "There's no hurry, child." She laid a gentle hand upon her arm. "Take all the time you need."

Miss Webster put her hand over her guardian's. "Thank you."

"You were all right on the tram," Lady Owston observed, recalling their proximity to the small steam locomotive's oven.

"The fire was obscured by the door for the most part," Miss Webster explained.

A girl in her late teens, wearing a maid's uniform, emerged from the open doorway. When the Bow Streeters looked to her, she gave a brief bob of her body and said, "I'm Lucy, Mrs Bloomingdale's maid. I've been told to fetch you some brandy."

Miss Webster parted her lips to decline, but Lady Owston spoke first, "Yes, thank you." Lady Owston guided Miss Webster toward the maid. "And if it's not too much trouble, a quiet corner where she may settle her nerves."

Miss Webster shot Lady Owston a hard look.

"I must return to Mrs Bloomingdale," Lady Owston said, returning inside.

Miss Webster stared after her in irritated disbelief.

"This way, miss," the maid said, indicating the door into the living room.

Miss Webster went into the room, albeit reluctantly, and sat in the offered armchair by the unlit fire. Whilst the maid poured her a small brandy, Miss Webster looked to the door and debated whether she should rejoin her guardian. Upon reflection, though, she realised Lady Owston may not have been acting entirely out of character after all. In fact, she thought her guardian had been a little devious by accepting the offer of help on Miss Webster's behalf.

"How long have you worked here, Lucy?" Miss Webster enquired once she'd taken the glass of brandy.

"Two years."

"Do you enjoy it?"

"Work's as good as any," Lucy replied, toying with her apron. Yet her gaze drifted to the window with a look of longing in her eyes.

"Are there any other servants?" Miss Webster enquired, having another sip of brandy.

"Only Miss Lauder. She's governess to Master Todd." Lucy dropped her apron and tidied the already impeccable fireplace. Slowing in her tidying as she glanced at Miss Webster, she enquired, "You've come all the way from London, then, miss?"

"We have." Miss Webster set her brandy aside. "Have you been to London?"

Lucy smiled weakly as she shook her head. "Not me, miss. I've not been past the station." She took a rag from her pocket and wiped along the mantelshelf. "I'd like to." She turned to the window, the wistfulness returning to her eyes. "See the world, too." She shrugged her shoulders and continued her dusting. "Stop talking foolish, Lucy."

"Is it, though?"

"Is it what?"

"Foolish."

"I shouldn't be talking about this, not to you, miss. You're the mistress' guest. You don't want to listen to me going on."

"I don't mind." Miss Webster picked up her brandy and indicated the door as she stood. "Is Miss Lauder here?"

Lucy nodded. "Giving lessons to Master Todd in the nursery, she is."

"Has she travelled?"

Lucy fell silent as she searched her memory. "I'd say so. Her dad was rich, I heard, but spent the money on drink and women, so she's got to work." She stuffed the rag into her pocket. "If that'll be all, miss, I have work that needs doing."

Miss Webster took a calling card from her purse and offered it to her. "In case you should ever find yourself in London."

A sadness passed over Lucy's gaze. "Not me, miss."

"Why not?"

Lucy looked at her. "I couldn't go to London."

"Not even for a well-paid position in the home of a respectable widow?"

Lucy stared at her.

"Give it some thought. I'll return tonight at nine o'clock to hear your decision," Miss Webster said and held out the glass. "Thank you for the brandy."

"Brandy?" Lucy enquired, still in a daze. Jolted from it upon noticing the glass, though, she swiftly took it with both hands. "You're welcome. Yes." She clutched the glass to her chest as if it would protect her. "No." She turned sharply toward the door. "I've got things to do, miss."

"Where are you going with that brandy?" a woman's angry voice demanded from the hall. Its owner entered the room immediately after, obliging Lucy to take several backward steps. In her late twenties, the newcomer had gaunt features, a slender figure, and dark-red hair. "Have you stolen it?" The hard gaze of her hazel eyes bore into Lucy as she snatched the glass from her, causing some of the brandy to spill upon the carpet. She grabbed Lucy by the shoulder and pushed her aside. "*Look* what you've *done*, you *stupid* girl!"

"Begging your pardon, Miss Lauder," Lucy mumbled with tears in her eyes.

"It was my fault," Miss Webster lifted her hand.

Miss Lauder looked at her. For a split second, her eyes were wide with a mixture of surprise and fear. The anger returned just as quickly, however. "And you are?"

"Miss Agnes Webster, a guest of your mistress," the Bow Streeter replied.

"Get back to your work," Miss Lauder ordered, casting a glare at Lucy.

"Yes, Miss Lauder," Lucy mumbled and hurried away.

Miss Lauder closed the door and set the brandy glass down upon the mantelshelf. "You shouldn't defend her. She isn't worthy of your kindness."

"She didn't steal the brandy," Miss Webster said in a firm tone. "Your mistress instructed her to bring it to me because I was feeling unwell."

"If it's not the brandy, it's the silver," Miss Lauder remarked. "Girls like her are all cut from the same cloth."

"And you aren't?" Miss Webster challenged.

Miss Lauder parted her lips to deny it but thought better of it. She was also a servant, after all. Lowering her head, she picked up the glass and headed for the door. "I have a pupil to teach."

"You were in Mrs Gove's employ until recently," Miss Webster called after her.

Miss Lauder halted, her hand upon the doorknob. She looked back over her shoulder at her. "Yes."

"May I ask why you are now in Mrs Bloomingdale's?"

"No." Miss Lauder opened the door.

"Was your dismissal necessary because of your letter?"

Again, Miss Lauder halted and looked over her shoulder at her. This time, though, the look of surprise and fear remained. "You know of it?"

"*We* do."

"We?"

"The Bow Street Society." Miss Webster stood with her in the doorway. Lowering her voice to barely above a whisper, she continued, "We have been hired by Mrs Gove to retrieve it from Mrs Bloomingdale's possession."

"Do you know its contents?"

"No," Miss Webster replied, causing the fear to drain from Miss Lauder's eyes. "Nor are we interested in them. We just want to give the letter to Mrs Gove."

Miss Lauder turned her head away. Her voice was strained with emotion as she said, "To burn it."

"Which would be her right, since Mrs Bloomingdale has been using it to manipulate her into attending her social gatherings," Miss Webster pointed out.

The volume of Miss Lauder's voice dropped. "I know."

"Will you help us get the letter to her, then?"

Miss Lauder looked at her sharply. "*No*." Her eyes were sad for all her expression was hard. "I will *not*, and if you get it by any means other than Mrs Bloomingdale giving it to you, I shall report you to Constable Grieg." She strode from the room, along the hallway, and up the stairs toward what Miss Webster presumed to be the nursery.

"Are you ready, dear?" Lady Owston enquired from the parlour.

Formulating a plan to retrieve the letter that evening, Miss Webster went to her guardian. "Absolutely."

V

As Miss Webster had anticipated, Mrs Bloomingdale had denied any wrongdoing to Lady Owston. According to Mrs Bloomingdale, it was a cruel deception on Mrs Gove's part, one intended to bring disgrace upon an upstanding member of the community. Both Miss Webster and Lady Owston agreed this was unlikely due to the simple fact Mrs Gove had travelled to London to seek the Bow Street Society's help instead of writing to Miss Trent. It was a tremendous amount of effort to perpetuate a simple lie— an unnecessary amount of effort if that were the case.

Therefore, Miss Webster was adamant she would see her plan through to acquire Miss Lauder's letter. Lady Owston was initially reluctant to allow her ward to face such a risk. Yet, after much arguing from Miss Webster, she was convinced it was the only way without enlisting the assistance of other Society members or the police. Both options were unrealistic, since the only member who could execute the task was Mr Locke, and he hadn't been seen in months, and they doubted Mrs Gove wanted the scandal of police involvement.

A few hours later, Miss Webster was admitted into the Bloomingdale's residence by Lucy, who quietly closed the front door behind her. Both women stood still and listened for the sound of anyone approaching the hallway. When neither heard anything, they allowed themselves to breathe, again.

"Have you come to a decision?" Miss Webster whispered.

"I want to, Miss, *honestly* I do," Lucy began.

"Then it's settled," Miss Webster said before the maid could say any more. "Gather your things. We're leaving for London tonight."

Lucy's eyes widened. "But-but what do I tell the mistress?"

"Lady Owston will write to her from London."

Lucy nibbled her lip as she glanced along the hallway and up the stairs.

"My offer shan't last forever," Miss Webster warned.

Seemingly making up her mind, Lucy untied her apron and took it with her as she quietly went upstairs.

Miss Webster remained in the hallway until Lucy moved out of sight. At which point she burst into action: hurrying across the hallway and into the parlour. She recalled seeing a bureau in the corner and, knowing ladies as she did, was confident she'd find Mrs Gove's letter there. Her eyes immediately adjusted to the darkness, allowing her to rummage in the drawers in a matter of seconds.

"*Stop* what you are doing at *once*," Miss Lauder demanded behind her.

Miss Webster turned with an envelope clutched to her breast.

Miss Lauder's glare was illuminated by the candle in her hand.

"I'm not leaving until I have the letter," Miss Webster calmly warned and turned back to the bureau to resume her search.

"I thought I'd *warned* you—" Miss Lauder began, crossing the room and setting the candle and its holder down upon the bureau.

"Why don't you want me to have it?" Miss Webster interrupted, firmly. "Surely, it matters not to you now. You have a new position, a new home. And, as you said earlier, Mrs Gove will undoubtedly burn it."

Miss Lauder's head was bowed. "I'm ashamed."

Miss Webster resumed her search. "I think there is more to it than that." She scanned the signatures of the letters she came across. "Were you having an affair with Mr Gove?"

"*No!*" Miss Lauder cried loudly. Immediately realising the potential consequence of raising her voice, she looked toward the door and listened. Fortunately, she heard no sound of anyone coming. Returning her attention to Miss Webster, she lowered her voice once more and continued, "I may be a mere governess, but I am *not* anyone's *mistress*." She straightened her back and lifted her chin. "He attempted to seduce me, but I resisted. I tried to tell Mrs Gove, but she would hear none of it." She dropped her gaze and bowed her head. In a quiet voice tinged with sadness, she went on, "She dismissed me the same day."

Miss Webster felt triumphant as she found Miss Lauder's signature at the bottom of the next letter in the pile. Returning the others to the bureau, she scanned the letter's contents. "You still tried to warn her, though."

Miss Lauder lifted her head and pursed her lips when she saw the letter. She gave a curt nod and half-whispered, "Yes. I was angry when I wrote it. I wanted to hurt her as she'd hurt me."

Miss Webster glanced at the letter, but there was no indication within it of the reasoning behind such a statement. "Hurt you? How?"

Miss Lauder perched upon the arm of the chair and, bowing her head, held her tightly clasped hands within her lap. "She'd taken Temprance away from me."

"Mrs Gove's daughter?"

"Yes." Miss Lauder bowed her head deeper. "I now know it was foolish of me to feel such a way. Temprance isn't my child. I had no right to make demands to her mother." She lifted her head and stared at the letter. "I should have never written it."

"May I take it?" Miss Webster enquired. "I'll make sure Mrs Gove burns it."

Miss Lauder gave a weak smile. "I don't think you will have to ask her twice."

Lucy appeared in the doorway. In her hand was a faded sheet with its corners tied into a knot. Her meagre possessions were held within. With wide eyes, she looked from Miss Webster to Miss Lauder and back again.

112

"You should also know I intend to take Lucy into Lady Owston's service," Miss Webster said. As she shifted her gaze to the maid, she added, "Tonight."

Miss Lauder looked over at Lucy, initially surprised. This soon shifted into an expression filled with regret, though. After a moment's silence, she said, "I haven't been very kind to you, Lucy. I was angry at myself, and I inflicted that anger upon you. I'm sorry." She stood and faced her. "I wish you the best in your new position." She looked to Miss Webster. "You had better leave before the master and mistress are awakened by our voices."

Miss Webster slipped the letter into her pocket and, going to Lucy, put her arm around hers. "Thank you, Miss Lauder. Your assistance will not go unrewarded."

"I ask for nothing but a peaceful and comfortable existence," Miss Lauder replied.

"Don't we all?" Lucy enquired, unconvinced by the governess' apology but not really caring since it was likely they'd never see each other, again.

"True," Miss Lauder replied with a weak smile. "Goodbye, Lucy."

Yet, Lucy was already halfway to the front door with Miss Webster at her side.

VI

Miss Trent wrinkled her nose at the overpowering smell of vinegar as Inspector John Conway drenched his chipped potatoes in it. Falling into step beside him as they walked away from the window of the small fried fish shop, she watched him shovel several of the soggy things into his mouth. Having met a stone's throw from Spitalfields Market on Princes Street in London's East End, the late hour didn't seem to matter to the many food vendors selling their wares from window and stall alike. Though they might not have been as crowded as during daylight hours, the little dark streets and alleyways around Spitalfields were nonetheless occupied by those seeking cheap sustenance.

"Want some?" Inspector Conway held out the paper-wrapped pile.

"No," Miss Trent replied, glancing at the vinegar on his dark-red beard.

Although only in his forty-third year, Inspector Conway's weathered complexion made him appear older. His attire of a knee-length black overcoat, dark-blue suit and tie, and white shirt were well-kept, whilst his black leather shoes were brushed and polished.

"Thank you," Miss Trent added.

Inspector Conway continued eating as they turned left onto Wood Street. Walking toward Church Street, with its imposing structure of Christ Church, he enquired between swallows, "You got the report for Jones?"

"I do." Miss Trent stepped into the darkened doorway of a closed shop as she pulled the file from the inside pocket. "We were able to successfully extract the compromising letter from Mrs Gove's would-be blackmailer."

"Good." Inspector Conway ate the remaining chips and screwed the paper into a ball, causing him to flinch in pain. Releasing a slow, deep breath, he stuffed the ball into his pocket.

"I wish you'd have those ribs looked at," Miss Trent said, concerned, as she looked upon his blackened eye and bruised face. It had only been a matter of days since she'd watched him box in the *Key & Lion*'s cellar.

"There's nowt they could do but bind 'em."

Miss Trent cast a worried glance over him but knew he couldn't be convinced. She decided to return to the matter at hand by folding back the skirt of her coat and unbuttoning a large pocket concealed within its lining. Taking the Mrs Gove progress report from it, she put her coat back in place and handed over the report.

As Miss Trent watched him read it, she recalled Mrs Gove's delight at being given Miss Lauder's letter. Lady Owston and Miss Webster had passed it into Miss Trent's possession when they'd returned to London. Miss Trent had been surprised to learn they'd acquired a new maid but hadn't wanted to probe too deeply into their agreement, since she suspected it was on the verge of being unethical. Yet, regardless of the means employed, they had succeeded in their assignment, and the Bow Street Society had been paid handsomely by Mrs Gove.

As Miss Lauder had predicted, Mrs Gove burnt the letter in the Society's hearth the moment she was given it. Unbeknownst to Mrs Gove, though, Miss Webster had deposited a copy of the letter into the Society's safe—just in case their client demanded her money back. Miss Trent hoped it wouldn't come to that but, if working for the Society had shown her nothing else, it was that life was full of surprises. Recalling Mrs Gove's hurried departure from the Society's parlour a few days before, Miss Trent once again thought, *Wonders never cease.*

The Case of the Cryptic Clues

I

It was the penultimate day of December, a time when the festivities of Christmas had waned, but the anticipation of a new year had yet to take hold. Miss Trent had always likened it to purgatory in her mind, albeit accompanied by the seasonal pleasures of roasted chestnuts and rich puddings. She'd returned from her Aunt Dorothea's the previous day and was grateful to be back in Bow Street. Savouring the peace of the Society's house from the comfort of its warm kitchen, she looked at Mr Callahan Skinner sitting opposite.

His upper lip and chin were clean shaven, and his neat, brown hair, although flecked with grey, had recently been cut. A hint of mint also lingered in the air, suggesting he'd chewed upon a leaf of that herb prior to his arrival. Even though he was impeccably dressed the rest of the year, Christmas had apparently brought out a greater desire to look his best, for his clothes lacked the usual signs of wear. These consisted of a criss-crossing, lapelled, chocolate-brown waistcoat, crisp white shirt with loose-fitting sleeves, chocolate-brown trousers, and a white cravat. The stiff, brown leather of his riding boots had also creaked as he'd walked, suggesting they were a recent acquisition.

Miss Trent had opted for practicality and comfort over style as she originally hadn't been expecting any visitors. Therefore, her attire consisted of plain A-line, dark-green skirts and white blouse. Her chestnut-brown hair was tied into a thick braid and coiled into a bun at the base of her skull, with two loose strands of corkscrew ringlets framing her face.

She filled their cups from the teapot and watched Mr Skinner add cream and sugar to the dark, steaming liquid. Her gaze flicked from his face to his arm and back again. It would've been distressing if he'd wounded his right arm, but the fact he wore a false hand on it meant he could've adapted easily. As it was, he'd wounded his fully functioning left. It was with a sharp pang of guilt, then, that she watched him attempt to lessen his pain by minimising his movement, resulting in an awkward execution of preparing his tea. All of it was an uncomfortable reminder of how the Society's recent case had ended.

Although Mr Skinner had insisted upon placing himself in harm's way, the ultimate decision to allow him to do so had rested with her. His employment as the bodyguard of Captain and Lady Mirrell meant he routinely faced danger. Miss Trent hadn't met the Mirrells or been informed of their reason for employing a private protector, but she doubted the risks Mr Skinner faced on their behalf were greater than those he'd faced for the Bow Street Society.

"How is your arm?" Miss Trent enquired with a hint of dread.

"It hurts, but the doctor t'inks it's not infected," Mr Skinner replied in his soft accent.

The corners of Miss Trent's mouth turned upward. "Good." Her dark-brown eyes shone with a lifting of her countenance. "I'm glad." She took a mouthful of tea and stood as she replaced the cup upon its saucer. "There was another reason for my invitation."

Mr Skinner's posture perked up at that. He watched her cross to a worktop by the sink and retrieve something. When she returned with a long, red box, he leaned forward and rested his natural hand upon the table in anticipation of opening it.

"It was on the porch when I collected this morning's post," Miss Trent said, putting the box before him. "It had been hand delivered."

Mr Skinner noted the box had no address or stamp.

"This was with it." Miss Trent laid a small, rectangular card upon the box. Written on it was, *For C.S.* "You're the only member with those initials."

Mr Skinner picked up the card and turned it over. The underside was blank.

"It's also perfumed," Miss Trent pointed out.

Mr Skinner held the card to his nose and detected the strong scent of jasmine.

The heart-shaped face of a young woman with a petite nose, hazel eyes, and flowing blond hair leapt into his mind's eye. The back of his throat tensed in an instant as a heaviness descended upon his chest, and time seemed to stop. The phantom sensation of long hair touching his cheek invaded his senses when his mind's eye glimpsed an intimate encounter he'd had many years ago. With his focus turned inward, he failed to hear Miss Trent's voice. It wasn't until she gave his arm a gentle shake that he was snapped back to reality.

Miss Trent studied Mr Skinner's agitated expression. "Callahan?"

Mr Skinner returned the card to the box and pushed them away. "I don't want it."

"But you haven't—"

"I don't care," Mr Skinner snapped.

Miss Trent sat bolt upright with a sharp tightening of her features.

"Sorry," Mr Skinner said upon noticing her reaction. Averting his gaze at the same time, he first looked to the box and then to his cup. "Jasmine perfume… I knew someone who wore it."

The tension eased from Miss Trent's face but remained in her shoulders. "And you suspect the box is from them?"

"If it's not, whoever sent it knows what happened," Mr Skinner pushed back his chair to increase the space between him and the box. "So, I still don't want it."

"What happened, Callahan?" Miss Trent softly enquired.

"Not'ing," Mr Skinner dismissed.

Miss Trent pursed her lips and released a slow, deep breath. Detecting the rigidness of his jaw, she knew it would be futile to attempt to coax the story from him. Therefore, she reached for the box instead. "May I open it?"

"When I've gone."

Miss Trent rested the box upon one hand whilst the other gripped its lid. "Aren't you a little curious about what's inside?"

Mr Skinner stared at the box for several moments before shifting his gaze to Miss Trent. Her inquiring look made him realise that, despite his better judgement, he did want to know.

"Open it," he said, immediately feeling nauseous.

Miss Trent lifted the lid in one fluid motion to reveal a dried spear thistle and a red rose resting upon a bed of white tissue paper.

Mr Skinner's gaze locked upon the flora as his stomach clenched.

A heartbeat later, he was on his feet and heading for the door.

Miss Trent ran after him, taking the box with her.

"I don't want it," Mr Skinner insisted as she caught up with him in the hallway.

"Why is a rose and thistle so significant to you?" Miss Trent put herself between him and the front door. "I know of *The Thrissill and the Rois*, but I doubt fourteenth-century poetry is a passion of yours." She replaced the lid. "Many taverns have borne the same name. Were you involved in a brawl at one of them?"

"*No*," Mr Skinner curtly replied.

Miss Trent held up the box. "*Why* is *this* so significant to you, Callahan?"

"It's none of your business." Mr Skinner glared at her. "Let me through."

119

Miss Trent returned his glare. "It *is* my business if it affects this Society and its members."

"I'm not your client," Mr Skinner retorted. "I don't have to tell you a *t'ing*."

Miss Trent released a loud, deep breath through her nose. She knew he was right, but that only increased her frustration. "No. You're not." She thrust the box toward him. "Take it with you, at least."

Mr Skinner snatched it from her.

"You know where we are if you need us," Miss Trent gently reminded him.

Yet, he left as soon as she'd stepped aside.

II

Mr Skinner aimed his Webley Mark I revolver into the darkness of his bedroom as a thunderclap exploded overhead. Realising the weather was the probable cause of his sudden awakening, he returned his revolver to his bedside table. Years spent protecting the Mirrells had conditioned him to be always on high alert. Consequently, he instinctively reached for his revolver and sat up at the smallest of sounds whenever he slept. Yet, he didn't pull the trigger until he was awake and aware of what, or whom, he was aiming at.

He lay upon his back, and the young woman's smiling, heart-shaped face immediately appeared in his mind's eye. The scent of jasmine in the air compelled him to retrieve the card from the table and hold it against his nose. As he closed his eyes and slowly inhaled the scent, his mind transported him to a sun-drenched morning and a small room above the *Thorn & Thistle* public house.

There was only a single bed for them to share, but sleeping was far from their minds. He was holding her, again, in two perfectly formed arms. At that time—long before the cannon had taken his hand—he was happy. The happiest he'd ever been.

Anabella. Her name was etched onto his heart.

Another thunderclap, followed by the pitter-patter of rain against his window, roused him from his daydream.

Darkness and solitude were waiting for him.

A sudden feeling of despair descended upon him as he recalled how it had ended with Anabella. The cruel words and intense emotions were as vivid to him now as they were then.

He sat up and, moving to the side of the bed, put his feet on the floor. With his natural hand clenched into a fist and his stump resting upon his thigh, he focused upon the outline of his door whilst fighting to suppress his sorrow.

The events of the day flashed through his mind.

The meeting with Miss Trent.

The difficulty he'd had sustaining conversations.

The way his thoughts had returned to the box over and over.

The near-overwhelming desire to be alone, coupled with immense fatigue.

His employers had assumed his wounded arm was the cause of his behaviour, so had insisted upon him staying in his room for the remainder of the afternoon and evening. They had guests coming later today and, perhaps selfishly, had wanted him at his best. He had given no protest to their order and obeyed it without question.

He stood and opened his window to take in some air.

Christmas had been spent at the Mirrells' country estate in Surrey. With Captain Mirrell due to sail in the first days of January, the household had returned to the usual residence on Hyde Vale in Greenwich. It was near to the Royal Naval School, a place close to the captain's heart, and the lush green spaces of Greenwich Park. Greenwich Station was also a short drive away, thus making for easy access to the hustle and bustle of central London and its docks.

The detached two-storey house was constructed in the first half of the century, thereby making it a relatively new build compared to the Mirrells' other home. The redness of its bricks remained vivid despite the soot perpetually in the air, and its white timbered windows and slate tiled roof were structurally sound.

At the commencement of his employment as the Mirrells' bodyguard, Mr Skinner had conducted a thorough inspection of the locks, doors, windows, and other entry/exit routes at both houses. The grounds and boundary walls of both hadn't escaped his scrutiny, either. At his recommendation, almost all the locks were updated, and additional ones added to the inside of certain interior doors, specifically the master bedroom, cellar, and study

122

(the latter holding the captain's charts and instructions from Royal Navy command).

Mr Skinner's bedroom was at the rear of the house, overlooking the small, square garden. Composed of gravel for the most part, with a square of lawn in the centre, the garden had a high wall around its perimeter. A gate in the right-hand corner closest to the house led to the service alleyway that ran adjacent to the property. Habitually scanning the garden for anything untoward, he took several deep, invigorating breaths before closing the window.

No sooner had he done so, did he notice a small, flashing ball of yellow light atop the garden wall's far-right corner. The heavy rain, combined with the thick clouds covering the moon, made it impossible for him to distinguish any figures in the darkness. He knew the alleyway went past there, so he concluded it was the likeliest entry point.

Although he was confused about their decision to remain atop the wall instead of entering the garden, he dismissed the idea they were signalling to an accomplice inside the house. He'd assisted Lady Mirrell in vetting the servants, and none had shown any cause for concern. Nevertheless, he had no choice but to concede they had been signalling *someone*—an accomplice on the garden's opposite side, perhaps? Resolving to uncover the truth, he pulled on his coat over his nightclothes, put on his boots, and collected his revolver as he strode from the room.

He emerged from the house just a few moments later, but despite his swiftness, the light had vanished. Perturbed, he checked the gate. Its bolt and padlock remained intact. Walking the perimeter next, he kept to the rear of the flowerbeds and held his revolver aloft as he focused on the wall's top edge with the occasional glance to the garden. The constant thud of the rain against the ground limited his ability to distinguish small sounds, however. Thus, he was obliged to rely upon his senses of touch and sight, neither of which presented him with anything untoward. All the while, he felt increasingly weighed down by his clothes as they became sodden from the rain.

When he finally reached the spot where he'd seen the light, he was half-relieved and half-confused to find it was deserted. All that appeared to remain was the lantern, its light shielded by a door in its side. He made a swift examination of it but found it had no distinguishing marks. Therefore, he set it on the ground to retrieve later.

After casting another glance over the garden and seeing no one and nothing, he took several steps back from the wall. He then slipped his revolver into his pocket before running and leaping forward. Hooking his natural arm over the top of the wall to catch himself, he dug the wooden fingers of his false hand into the brickwork and pulled himself up to peer into the alleyway beyond. Again, he saw no one and nothing.

Why were they here? He wondered, lowering himself back over the wall and dropping to the ground. Catching the glint of something dropping onto the ground at the same time, he retrieved the lantern and used its light to examine the flowerbed immediately around him. Almost at once, it landed on a silver ring half-hidden in the mud. Plucking it from the ground, Mr Skinner held it near to the lantern's candle to examine it more closely.

It can't be, he thought, feeling a sudden coldness in his core and a tightening of his stomach as he gazed upon the ring's engraving of a perpetual vine. He turned it over and over, reluctant to acknowledge the idea niggling at the periphery of his mind. Inevitably, it pushed its way through. *This is Anabella's ring.* Nausea crept into his consciousness. *The one Mághnus gave to her when he proposed.*

III

Sleep had eluded Mr Skinner for the remainder of the night. The thistle, rose, and ring appeared to hint at a series of events which had happened over ten years ago. The question of why kept popping into his mind, but he couldn't think of a satisfactory answer. The connected question of who had also plagued his thoughts. It was evident *someone* knew what happened, but he'd not spoken of the events for almost nine years.

Rising before dawn, as was his habit, he'd conducted his usual patrol of the house and garden before sharing breakfast with the servants in the kitchen. Next, he'd kept silent watch over the Mirrells as they'd breakfasted, and then accompanied Lady Mirrell to the library.

Standing in the corner whilst she wrote some letters, he'd allowed his gaze to drift to the oil painting hung upon the chimney breast. It depicted HMS Valiant, the vessel Captain Mirrell had served as commander on for much of his naval career.

Mr Skinner had served under him for the entirety of his own short career. Like many others, he'd started as a cabin boy. After progressing to the position of sailor within a few months, he'd then shown impressive competence when assisting the gunnery lieutenants and sub-lieutenants in their work. Responsible for the maintenance and operation of the guns and safe storage of the ammunition onboard HMS Valiant, these officers had been trained at the Royal Naval School.

Although a keen and natural-born sailor, Mr Skinner had lacked the connections and wealth which would've allowed him to follow in their footsteps. Nevertheless, the immense respect and trust he'd earned from Captain Mirrell, and others, led to his promotion to a bosun's mate, a petty officer responsible for supervising the seamen's everyday duties. He was never far away from the gun deck, though, and unfortunately, it was this passion and dedication that caused him to be in the wrong place at the wrong time.

Mr Skinner glanced at his false hand as it rested upon his knee. Lady Mirrell had received a message whilst writing her letters, one that had obliged her to send him on an errand. The Mirrells' guests, Lord and Lady Clairmont, were expected around noon for luncheon. Lord Clairmont had been summonsed back to central London, however, leaving Lady Clairmont and her companion to make the railway journey alone. He had written ahead, though, expressing his heartfelt desire that his wife be met at Greenwich Station and escorted to the Mirrell residence on Hyde Vale. Neither the station nor the neighbourhood were known for being the hunting grounds of thieves and ne'er-do-wells, but as Lord Clairmont stated in his message, it would "bring me great peace of mind to know Lady Clairmont was adequately protected on the final part of her journey." Thus, Mr Skinner was sent in the Mirrells' carriage to carry out this duty.

As the vehicle trundled through the streets, Mr Skinner's thoughts returned to HMS Valiant, Annabella, and the ring. He and Mághnus Robbins had joined the royal navy at the same time. Yet, while Mr Skinner showed a natural aptitude for life on the seven seas, Mághnus was plagued by sickness. Mr Skinner had done all he could to support his friend, though, and, after a year, Mághnus finally gained his sea legs.

Mághnus had also met Annabella Doon, the beautiful daughter of the Valiant's midshipman. They seemed to have fallen in love at first sight, and Mághnus spent all his shore leave in her company. Somehow, they'd managed to keep their courtship a secret from Annabella's father. As Mághnus's best friend, Mr Skinner was one of the few people who knew. In fact, he'd often acted as go-between for the lovers.

On one occasion, when he was delivering Mághnus' latest love letter to Annabella, things changed between her and Mr Skinner. She was upset about being apart from Mághnus, and Mr Skinner had offered her comfort. He had only intended for it to be an embrace, but when they'd looked into each other's eyes, they'd recognised a mutual longing. It was just a kiss, at first, but neither of them could end their meeting there. They made love that night, in the small room above the *Thorn & Thistle* public house.

Mághnus never knew the truth.

Mr Skinner and Annabella met several times, again, after that. Each time in secret, each time in the small room above the *Thorn & Thistle*. They were in love, but they loved Mághnus, too. Neither wanted to break his heart. Mr Skinner suspected it was the reason why Annabella agreed to elope with Mághnus. She hadn't told him of their plans, so it had come as quite a shock to hear Mághnus whisper them to him by the fire at the *Thorn & Thistle*. He'd looked to Annabella for an answer, but she averted her gaze. With hindsight, he could see the impossible situation she was in: she loved them both, but only Mr Skinner was strong enough to withstand the pain of losing her.

Mr Skinner had returned to HMS Valiant with a shattered heart that night.

Mághnus and Annabella eloped in the early hours of the morning.

Mr Skinner didn't see either again until almost a year later.

The Mirrells' carriage slowed to a stop, and Mr Skinner looked out to see the two-storey building of Greenwich Station. Constructed from greyish yellow brick, it had stood on this site for as long as Mr Skinner could remember. It wasn't as grand as King's Cross or Euston, but its modest platforms and buildings were clean and functional.

Alighting from the carriage, Mr Skinner exchanged a few words with the driver in which the latter informed him he would do a loop around the station to keep the horse's muscles loose. By the time Mr Skinner would emerge with Lady Clairmont and her companion, the driver would've returned. Agreeing to the arrangement, Mr Skinner went into the station and headed for the ladies' waiting room.

Finding it contained two occupants upon entering, he looked to the woman in her early twenties first since she was sitting the closest. Catching movement beside her, he shifted his gaze to the second woman and went completely still when he saw her heart-shaped face. The sounds of the station also became muffled, like he was under water. "It can't be…" he muttered, moving his gaze up and down her as she stood and walked toward him.

"It is good to see you, Callahan," she said, the sound of her voice invoking the old emotions within his heart as he struggled to follow his swirling thoughts. Feeling as though he were paralysed at the same time, he could only stare at her as she stood a couple of feet away from him. Without taking her eyes off him, she issued instructions to the younger woman. "Stand by the door, Charlotte. Ensure we are not disturbed."

"Yes, my lady," the younger woman agreed and left the waiting room to stand guard outside.

"Annabella," Mr Skinner half-whispered, afraid she'd vanish if he said it any louder.

"Yes, Callahan," Annabella said, slowly closing the distance. "It's me."

Mr Skinner darted his gaze to the empty seats, to the wall, and back to her. "What are you doin' here? Why are you—?" He shook his head and turned away as he struggled to get a grip upon his thoughts. "The box… the ring… all of it was you."

"Yes." Annabella lowered her head but only momentarily broke her gaze from his. "I did not want you to be surprised when I—"

"*Surprised*?!" Mr Skinner cried, staring at her in disbelief. "You've come back into my life after almost nine *years*, Annabella. I'm a bit more than '*surprised.*'" He turned sideways and, pointing at the door, looked between it and her as he demanded, "And why send her out? Did you t'ink we were goin' to fall into each other's arms?"

"What I have to say is for your ears alone, Callahan," Annabella replied firmly.

Mr Skinner turned his back and headed for the door. "I don't have time for this. I have to meet Lady Clairmont."

"I *am* Lady Clairmont," Annabella called after him.

Mr Skinner stopped, his hand upon the doorknob. He looked over his shoulder at her. "*You're* Lady Clairmont?"

"Yes," Annabella replied.

Mr Skinner turned to face her but remained within easy reach of the exit.

"Do you see why I wanted to warn you of my coming?" Annabella continued. "If I had arrived at the Mirrell residence without doing so, you would have reacted as you are now, and I could not bear to be the cause of your dismissal. I have hurt you already. I did not want to do so again."

Mr Skinner moved forward and only then noticed the ring on her wedding finger and the finery of her clothes. The memory of witnessing Mághnus proposing to her at the *Thorn & Thistle* flooded his mind's eye as the old pain gripped his heart. *He'd* wanted her to be *his* after Mághnus had… *Poor Mághnus*, he lamented, thinking of his friend's smiling face and then his skull infested with maggots. Pushing the distressing image aside, he recalled another of his life's worst moments instead. "I asked you to marry me once."

"I remember," Annabella said in a subdued voice.

A heavy silence descended between them as their minds replayed that fateful day, each recalling the details differently.

"I said certain things I regret to this day," Annabella admitted.

"Do you regret sayin' no?"

Annabella briefly pursed her lips as she considered lying to him. Deciding she'd come too far to tell him anything but the truth, she replied, "No. Not anymore."

Mr Skinner closed the distance between them. "But you did?"

"Once."

Mr Skinner stopped abruptly, as if he'd been shot.

"But then I fell in love with Christopher," Annabella said. "Lord Clairmont."

Mr Skinner turned away and walked slowly to the seats, his shoulders slouched, and his hand clenched into a fist at his side. The pain and sorrow boiled within his breast, but he was adamant he wouldn't show her such weakness.

Annabella stood behind him, her wrists against her stomach as her right thumb rubbed the knuckle of her left index finger. Her pleading eyes were also bright with regret. "I know you were not the one who betrayed us to Captain Mirrell."

Mr Skinner immediately turned around and glared at her. "Have you decided to believe me now, then?"

"I deserve your anger."

Mr Skinner walked away, across the room.

Annabella watched him as, in a voice strained with emotion, she continued, "I have since learned it was Mr Woodcroft, the landlord of the *Thorn & Thistle*. He was a retired sailor who had served under Captain Mirrell and…" She stopped herself and momentarily bowed her head. "That is not important now. What is important is you knowing how deeply I regret the cruel way I treated you."

"You called me a cripple," Mr Skinner said, his hard voice echoing the tension in his jaw. Yet, there was a clear sorrow in his eyes. "You said I couldn't be the man Mághnus was to you."

"He had just died from exhaustion in prison, doing the hard labour the navy had sentenced him to for desertion. We were lovers. What else could I have thought under the circumstances other than you had betrayed Mághnus so you could have me for yourself?"

"I *swore* on the bible I hadn't," Mr Skinner insisted. "But it wasn't enough for you, Annabella." A pained look passed over his face. "*I* wasn't enough for you." He gestured to her clothes. "This proves it."

"Yes." Annabella's gaze was sympathetic even though her reply was not. "It does."

Mr Skinner turned away as his heartache intensified to an unbearable level. He glanced at the door, contemplating a swift exit. He could walk away, force himself to forget this conversation, and deny to himself that he'd seen her.

Yet, aside from hating himself for even considering a retreat, he still had a duty to fulfil. Lady Mirrell had instructed him to accompany her guest to the house for luncheon and, despite everything, he refused to renege on his responsibilities. He survived losing Annabella before, he would do so again.

"What is it you want from me?" he enquired in a softened tone as he met her gaze.

"Forgiveness, but if that is too much to ask for, then—"

"You're forgiven."

Unconvinced of the sincerity of his swift answer, Annabella began, "Callahan—"

"That's all I'm willin' to give."

Annabella closed her mouth and, giving a small nod, gathered her emotions. Locking them away in a part of her heart that would never be reopened, she stood tall and said in a formal tone, "Then our time here is spent, Mr Skinner." Walking past him, she left the waiting room.

He watched her through the window and felt his heartache ease. A newfound sense of relief also took its place and, as he recalled her parting words, he realised he'd had the absolution he'd been seeking all these years.

"That it is, Annabella," he softly said aloud.

Finally. He was free.

Enjoyed the book? Please show your support by writing a review.

DISCOVER MORE AT...
www.bowstreetsociety.com

Notes from the author

Spoiler alert

At the time of writing, this sixth volume of the Bow Street Society Casebook is being completed a year later than planned. It's staggering to think how much my life has changed in a single year. I remember listening to the audio version of *The Case of Mastermind Moss* from the fifth volume with my mum in her living room. She was astounded at the complexity of the plot and amazed at how I'd been able to come up with it. We both agreed Richard A. Boxshall's delivery as the narrator was spot on, too. (You can listen to it on the Bow Street Society YouTube channel). Sadly, my mum passed away in February of this year (2023). She was a major part of my life, so, we (my family and I) were utterly devastated when we lost her. I've found writing difficult since then. Yet, I know she would've wanted me to continue.

If you've read volumes 1-5 of the Bow Street Society Casebook, you'll be familiar with the formula each story usually follows:

1) a client explains their case to Miss Trent.
2) the assigned Society members question the client.
3) these members investigate.
4) the Society delivers its conclusions.

You may have noticed, then, the stories in this sixth volume are a significant departure from this formula (*The Case of the Bold Blackmailer* being the exception). I enjoy writing short stories as they are an opportunity to experiment with my own troupes whilst exploring the Bow Street Society universe and its characters. In this sixth volume, I experimented and explored further than I have previously. I'm delighted with the results, and I hope you are, too.

The Case of the Scream in the Smog

The opening of this story is an immediate deviation from the formula. Not only is Miss Trent absent, but Mr O'Mooney doesn't even become the Society's client after hearing the scream in the smog. Instead, Mr Keegan Alan, the porter at Peabody Square, enlists the Society's help under the orders of Superintendent Dougal Reid who, in turn, is acting on behalf of the Peabody Donation Fund. Although the roles of porter and superintendent existed within the Peabody Donation Fund organisation of the time, the characters are fictional. This was a conscious decision on my part as I wanted to avoid referencing real people when I hadn't gained the permission to do so from their descendants. I was supported in my decision by the official historian at the Peabody Trust, Christine Wagg.

In February 2022, I interviewed Christine for the Bow Street Society blog at a time when the story was being serialised in the *Gaslight Gazette*. Christine's intimate, expert knowledge of not only Peabody Square, but all Peabody dwellings and the trust's history, was invaluable. The floorplans, photographs, testimonies, and critique she graciously gave to me were vital to ensuring my portrayal of Peabody Square (its interior & exterior, the nature of those who lived & worked there, its rules, etc.) was as faithful to the reality of the place in 1896 as possible.

My inspiration for *The Case of the Scream in the Smog* came from an entry in a collection of Victorian detective stories I'd purchased from a charity shop. The entry featured a well-to-do gentleman leaving his social club to walk home in a smog. Like Mr O'Mooney, the gentleman is faced with a yellow, sooty smog so thick he is unable to distinguish buildings or other landmarks. Obliged to feel along the walls of buildings to find his way, the gentleman makes good progress on his journey, until he is confronted by others approaching from the opposite direction. When it becomes apparent they can't pass each other whilst still holding onto the building, the gentleman does the polite thing and moves out of the way. Unfortunately, after the others have passed, he becomes disorientated and consequently lost.

The image of foggy, cobbled streets is a cliché synonymous with Victorian London. Yet we, as readers, picture the white, wispy kind most of all. I wanted to avoid this cliché and present the dirty, suffocating smog Londoners regularly endured instead. Furthermore, I wanted the reader to feel as though they were Mr O'Mooney, hence the description of his experience through his senses.

As with other Bow Street Society stories, the route Mr O'Mooney takes from the train station (including the street names) is based upon maps from the time. I did this to further add to the sense of place within the story, thereby ensuring the reader is fully transported back to 1896. Peabody Square still stands today as the home of many Londoners. It also remains the property of the Peabody Trust.

If you've read *The Case of the Toxic Tonic* and *The Case of the Maxwell Murder* from the Bow Street Society Mystery series, you would've made the connection about Constable Caulfield that Dr Locke did. *The Case of the Scream in the Smog* was written before *The Case of the Pugilist's Ploy* and before I'd made the decision to promote him between the fifth and sixth novels. Hence why he is only a constable in *The Case of the Scream in the Smog*, instead of a sergeant as stated in *The Case of the Pugilist's Ploy*.

The Case of the Impossible Implication

This story deviates from the formula in its structure. Whereas Casebook stories usually follow a linear plotline, *The Case of the Impossible Implication* is told in reverse. The chapter headings are also a deviation from the formula. Their purpose was twofold: firstly, to assist the reader in keeping track of what is going on, and secondly, to honour the Victorian tradition of including explanatory headings before each chapter.

My inspiration for *The Case of the Impossible Implication* was the film *Memento*, released in 2000. In it, Guy Pearce plays Leonard Shelby, an ex-insurance investigator suffering from anterograde amnesia. The amnesia causes him to have short-term memory loss and an inability to form new memories. There are two storylines within the movie, one told in a linear fashion, and the other is told backwards. With each new scene of this second storyline, the viewer is given a little more about what's really going on. The result of watching the two storylines are feelings of confusion and disorientation which are only alleviated when we are taken back to the very beginning, and the truth is finally revealed. The backward storytelling means that, although it is the beginning of the story, we have reached the end of the film. It is one of the cleverest films I've ever seen, and I highly recommend it.

My decision to place *The Case of the Impossible Implication* in a school was based upon my desire to explore the other side of Mr Virgil Verity, that being his past career as a schoolmaster. Opportunities to do this was the opening scene, and the knowledge Mr Verity draws upon to solve the case. Hampstead Public School is fictional, but its appearance, etc, was based upon real public schools of the time.

If you've read the Bow Street Society Mystery books, you may have recognised the doctor, referred to by Mr Verity, who specialises in illnesses of the mind. It is, of course, Dr Neal Colbert, who is introduced in *The Case of the Maxwell Murder.* Mental health conditions weren't as understood as they are now. Therefore, although Dr Colbert would've been a highly respected doctor at his asylum, he would've had little to go on as far as Mr Waller's condition and treatment were concerned. Being

as sympathetic to his fellow man as he is, though, Dr
Colbert would've done all within his power to help.

The Case of the Lyall Lighthouse

This story deviates from the formula in its location and
length. Unlike other Casebook stories, it is based in
Scotland and contains seven chapters. *The Case of the
Lyall Lighthouse* was heavily influenced by my research.
The choice of location was based upon what I'd learned
about lighthouses (their construction, ownership, etc), who
managed them (lightkeepers, etc.) and how (maintaining
the light, etc.). This research largely comprised of the non-
fiction book *The Lighthouse: The Mystery of the Eilean
Mor Lighthouse Keepers* by Keith McCloskey.

    The Banshee Inn where Dr Weeks, Mr Heath, and
Mr Skinner first meet Superintendent Roy was fictional.
The harbour at Cutcloy was a real place, however. I chose
the harbour as the nearest landmark because I wanted to
use a fictional lighthouse, and I knew there wasn't one
near the harbour in 1896. Furthermore, it is on the west
coast of Scotland, the side closest to the Atlantic and its
shipping routes.

    Like the Peabody Donation Fund in *The Case of
the Scream in the Smog*, the Northern Lighthouse Board,
its business address, the positions within it, and the duties
performed by its employees are based upon historical fact.
Again, like the characters in *The Case of the Scream in the
Smog*, I used fictional individuals to avoid depicting real
people without the consent of their descendants. I was
careful to give the characters Scottish names, however, as I
wanted to remain true to the country and its people.

    My inspiration was the poem *Flannan Isle* by
Wilfrid Wilson Gibson, published in 1912. I first read it in
an anthology during a GCSE English Literature class at
school. The image of the overturned chair, the laid table,
and empty lighthouse stayed with me long after I'd read
the piece, especially after learning it was based on a true

story. Therefore, when I decided I wanted to base a Casebook story in a lighthouse, my thoughts returned to the poem. I did some research into the poem's origins and, upon discovering it was based on the Eilean Mor lighthouse mystery, sought out more information. This led me to Keith McCloskey's book.

My original idea was to place Mr Verity, Mr Elliott, and Dr Locke in a lighthouse that had been mysteriously abandoned by its keepers. There was going to be a suggestion their disappearance was supernatural in nature, and, so, I planned to have Mr Elliott (the sceptic) clash with Mr Verity (the believer) with Dr Locke acting as mitigator. I couldn't come up with a satisfactory solution to the disappearance, however. Especially since there would've been no witnesses and very little evidence for the Bow Streeters to analyse. Therefore, I decided to reduce the missing keepers to one, keep two other keepers around for the Bow Street Society to question, and replace Dr Locke, Mr Verity, and Mr Elliott with Dr Weeks, Mr Heath, and Mr Skinner.

The Case of the Bold Blackmailer

The only story to adhere to the formula, it begins with Miss Trent and Miss Dexter in the kitchen at Bow Street and ends with Miss Trent meeting Inspector Conway near Spitalfields, London. If you've read *The Case of the Pugilist's Ploy* you may have recognised these scenes. The placement of them in this short story was intentional, as I wanted to bring the timelines of both series (Casebook and Mystery) together.

My original intentional was to include the opening scene from *The Case of the Christmas Crisis* in the prologue of *The Case of the Pugilist's Ploy*. Unfortunately, the timeline of the short story was too close to Christmas Day to allow me to squeeze in the events of the novel. Therefore, I had to resort to creating a new client and case to fit the opening scene. I also had to change some of the

140

details. For example, in *The Case of the Christmas Crisis*, Miss Trent and Miss Dexter are making decorations. Whereas in *The Case of the Pugilist's Ploy,* Miss Trent is making minced pies, and Miss Dexter is sketching. As I was obliged to make the scene change for plot purposes, I decided to write the short story to fit the scene in the novel—*The Case of the Bold Blackmailer*.

The main part of the story occurs in Wolverton, Buckinghamshire as it is an area I'm very familiar with. Today, it is one of the eight towns and villages which were encompassed by the City of Milton Keynes. In 1896, though, it was a standalone place at the centre of England's railway industry.

The white train station described in the story was still standing when I was a child. I vaguely remember going down its steps to the platform when my mum, my siblings, and I travelled to Sunderland via Birmingham New Street. It was demolished a few years later, though, and a new station now stands at the foot of the hill. Other real-life features of Wolverton which I included in the story were the steam tramway, Cambridge Street, and Windsor Street. Today, Wolverton is largely protected by conservation rules. Therefore, many of the Victorian-era terraced houses are not only still standing but continue to be occupied by families.

Aside from books written by local historians, I've encountered Wolverton in other literary works only once: in *The Suspicions of Mr Whicher* by Kate Summerscale. In it, she describes how Inspector Whicher travels to Wolverton train station to follow up on a lead that a local man has confessed to the Road Hill House murder. A crowd has gathered on the platform to meet the famous detective from Scotland Yard. It soon becomes apparent to Whicher, though, that the man is lying.

The Case of the Cryptic Clues

This story deviates from the formula in that the Bow Street Society member assigned (Mr Skinner) is also the mystery at its centre. Consequently, the reader becomes the detective uncovering the truth about the clues Mr Skinner finds—a truth he knows but is reluctant to reveal. There isn't a crime in the story, either and the only problem is the unknown identity of the person leaving the clues.

My inspiration came from a short scene in *The Case of the Pugilist's Ploy* in which Mr Skinner sees Mrs Farley for the first time. He has an inward monologue about her reminding him of a past love and the painful memories attached to them. I wanted to build upon this aspect of Mr Skinner's character as, apart from his role as the Mirrells' bodyguard and the circumstances around the loss of his hand, little is known about him away from the Bow Street Society. I therefore conducted research into the rules regulating the Royal Navy at the time of Mr Skinner's service and, from this, formulated the story around his past love.

Yet rather than being a love story in which Mr Skinner rekindles a romance with his one true love, it's a story about redemption and freeing oneself from the pain of the past. When Mr Skinner leaves the waiting room, he has an intense feeling of relief, as he has carried around the guilt about his best friend for years. Now, though, he can start afresh as he's finally laid that ghost to rest.

I dedicated *The Case of the Pugilist's Ploy* to my mum because she loved boxing. I want to take this moment to dedicate this sixth volume of Casebook stories to her, too. She always believed in me and my writing. I promised her I would live the best life I could and make the Bow Street Society series a success. I'm determined to keep my promise, and I appreciate your support in helping me to do that.

~ **T.G. Campbell,** *October 2023*

MORE BOW STREET SOCIETY

**The Case of The Shrinking Shopkeeper
& Other Stories**
(Bow Street Society Casebook Volume 1)

An illusionist, medical doctor, veterinary surgeon,
architect, freelance journalist, solicitor, artist, cabman,
secretary, and newspaper journalist are all called upon by
the Society's clerk, Miss Rebecca Trent, to investigate a
plethora of peculiar puzzles. From a sweet-shop owner
who believes he's losing height at an alarming rate to the
mysterious disappearance of a woman from inside a
carriage. From a beloved family pet being the subject of a
bizarre accusation, to a conversation with a dead man, to
an unjust dismissal from a toy maker's. Each Bow Street

Society member must draw upon their knowledge and expertise to solve these baffling problems once and for all…

In this collection:

The Case of the Shrinking Shopkeeper
The Case of the Winchester Wife
The Case of the Perilous Pet
The Case of the Eerie Encounter
The Case of the Christmas Crisis

On sale now in eBook and paperback from Amazon.
Also available for free download via Kindle Unlimited.

The Case of The Peculiar Portrait
& Other Stories
(Bow Street Society Casebook Volume 2)

In this second volume, the Bow Street Society investigates
more baffling problems posed by a colourful array of
clients. Can a crime be solved before it's committed? How
have people fallen from a window that can't be opened?
How has a dead man disappeared from his own portrait?
These are just some of the questions the Bow Street
Society must answer to expose the fantastic truths behind
these bizarre cases.

In this collection:

The Case of the Desperate Deed
The Case of the Scandalous Somnambulist
The Case of the Chilling Chamber
The Case of the Ghastly Gallop
The Case of the Peculiar Portrait

On sale now in eBook and paperback from Amazon.
Also available for free download via Kindle Unlimited.

**The Case of The Russian Rose
& Other Stories
(Bow Street Society Casebook Volume 3)**

The Case of the Russian Rose & Other Stories is the third volume of shorter mysteries to feature the group. Wherein they must solve peculiar problems posed by their colourful array of clients, such as: "how is a pocket picked in an empty train compartment?" and "How did a bullet vanish from a gun without being fired?" These are just some of the questions the Bow Street Society must answer to expose the fantastic truths behind these bizarre cases

In this collection:

The Case of the Pesky Passenger
The Case of the Taken Teacup
The Case of the Russian Rose
The Case of the Crooked Cottage
The Case of the Baffled Bride

On sale now in eBook and paperback from Amazon.
Also available for free download via Kindle Unlimited.

**The Case of The Gentleman's Gambit
& Other Stories**
(Bow Street Society Casebook Volume 4)

The Case of the Gentleman's Gambit & Other Stories is
the fourth volume of shorter mysteries to feature the
group. Wherein they must solve peculiar problems posed
by their colourful array of clients, such as: "how did gold
vanish from a moving train without four guards seeing the
thief?", "Is a ghost from Whitechapel haunting a wealthy
woman?" and "Can playing cards be used to poison
someone?" These are just some of the questions the Bow
Street Society must answer to expose the fantastic truths
behind these bizarre cases.

In this collection:

The Case of the Terrific Theft
The Case of the Whitechapel Wraith
The Case of the Fowler Fortune
The Case of the Gentleman's Gambit
The Case of the Puma Problem

On sale now in eBook and paperback from Amazon.
Also available for free download via Kindle Unlimited.

The Case of The Fearful Father
& Other Stories
(Bow Street Society Casebook Volume 5)

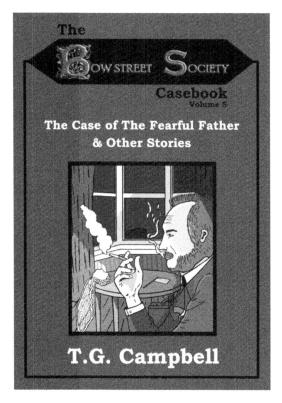

The Case of The Fearful Father & Other Stories is the
fifth volume of shorter mysteries to feature the group.
Wherein they must solve peculiar problems posed by their
colourful array of clients, such as: "how is a thief using
newspaper advertisements to commit his crimes?", "How
did a burglar disappear from a locked room?" and "What
made a teetotaller violently sick during a visit to the Blue
Lily?" These are just some of the questions the Bow Street
Society must answer to expose the fantastic truths behind
these bizarre cases.

In this collection:

The Case of Mastermind Moss
The Case of the Counterfeit Clairvoyant
The Case of the Doomed Drawlatch
The Case of the Fearful Father
The Case of the Redi Robbery

On sale now in eBook and paperback from Amazon.
Also available for free download via Kindle Unlimited.

SOURCES OF REFERENCE

Research has been conducted into the various historical aspects of the fictional stories contained within this collection. These aspects include, but are not limited to, geographical information, the interior & exterior appearances of real locations, and the workings of real organisations. In this section, I cite the facts and sources which have been used to directly inform these aspects. Each citation includes the origin and author of a source, and which part or story it relates to. All rights connected to the sources remain with their respective authors and publishers.

The Case of the Scream in the Smog

The following sources were gratefully received from Christine Wagg, Historian at The Peabody Trust. Christine also provided historical context for each source and graciously took the time to proofread the historical accuracy of the representation of Peabody Square, Shadwell, in the story.

Shadwell estate layout plan before Glamis Place added (1935)
Proximity of the gate into Peabody Square to Charles Place, the layout of Peabody Square, the direction the blocks faced, the name of the south block, the fact the blocks were detached.

PEABODY-SQUARE, SHADWELL article from the Illustrated London News, (23rd February 1867)
The 'Peabody Square' name.

Peabody Donation Fund. Instructions to Superintendents, (January 1912)
Mr O'Mooney's question about the gas being lit. Mr Alan getting paid overtime to do gate duty at Superintendent

Alan's order. The arrangement of Porters working under a Superintendent. The duty of the Porter to hose down the yard. The reference to the type of paint on the walls and ceiling in the south block.

Wagg, Christine <u>Shadwell estate: a brief summary of its history</u>, (2021)
The year Peabody Square was completed.

<u>The Thirty-Second Annual Report of the Trustees of the Peabody Donation Fund</u> for 1896 (February 1897)
Mr Heath's comment that the construction costs of Peabody Square were met by the Peabody Donation Fund and that they had continued to manage it to that day. The reference to the tenant Mr O'Mooney being a coachman and the tenant Mr Caulfield being a police constable based upon the list of occupations held by the heads of households residing in Peabody dwellings.

<u>Peabody Donation Fund. Shadwell Estate. Plan of North Block</u> (November 1935)
There is a note on this plan that states "South, East & West Blocks Similar." Used as the basis of the various descriptions of the internal layout of the south block.

The following references are based upon the information found on the corresponding pages of Wagg, Christine, and McHugh, James, <u>Homes for London: The Peabody Story</u> (Peabody, London, 2017):

Blurb on Rear Cover
Mr Heath's reference to Mr George Peabody's name, nationality, occupation, and status as a philanthropist.

Page 21
Mr Heath's reference to the Parliamentary report in 1885 that recorded a two-year waiting list for a Peabody dwelling.

Page 13

Dr Locke's reference to several of her poorer patients applying to the waiting list for a Peabody dwelling but being refused on the basis they were unemployed or worked on the markets. Also, Mr Heath's response that the Peabody Donation Fund relies on the rent from tenants to fund the maintenance, and his assumption that the fund would run dry without the tenants' rent.

Photograph of Shadwell Estate, p.104
The description of the blocks' yellow bricks was based upon their appearance in this photograph.

***

Charles Booth's London Poverty maps and police notebooks
https://booth.lse.ac.uk/
The description of Mr O'Mooney's route from Mercer Street, along Shadwell High Street, and eventually to Charles Place based upon the above map. The geographical location of the East London Hospital for Sick Children given in the story, including the names of the nearby streets, were also based upon the above map.

NORTH BLOCK WITH ATTACHED RAILINGS AND GATEPIERS PEABODY ESTATE entry on the Historic England website
https://historicengland.org.uk/listing/the-list/list-entry/1246616
The description of the blocks having slate roofs and timber windows was based upon the description of the architecture given in the above entry.

Records of the EAST LONDON HOSPITAL FOR CHILDREN AND DISPENSARY FOR WOMEN, Glamis Road, Shadwell, London, National Archives
https://discovery.nationalarchives.gov.uk/details/r/24065ff
e-9599-437e-9fa1-3b6647fc932d
The name of the hospital given in the story was based upon this entry. The "Administrative / biographical background" section of this entry also informed the assumption that the hospital would have occupied the Glamis Road site in 1896.

East London Hospital for Children in Shadwell. London. Henry and Charles Legg. 1877. Inscribed "FW" lower left. Source: Internet Archive web version of Illustrated London News (12 May 1877): 444. From the Victorian Web website
https://victorianweb.org/art/architecture/hospitals/6.html
The description of the East London Hospital was based upon this illustration. The fact that the hospital occupied this site from 1877 based upon the original text that accompanied the illustration in the Illustrated London News on 12th May 1877.

Gray, Henry, 1825-1861; Spitzka, Edward Anthony, 1876-1922 Anatomy, descriptive and applied (Published 1913)
https://archive.org/details/anatomydescript00gray
"Fig, 95. —Base of the skull. Interior View." on p.125 of this book used for name and description of the occipital bone and its location.

Page, M.D., David W. The Howdunnit Series: Body Trauma: A Writer's Guide to Wounds and Injuries, (Writer's Digest Books, Cincinnati and Ohio, 1996) pp.65-66
Description of bruising around Miss Fairclough's eyes. This is in reference to the "Raccoon eyes" term and its definition detailed in the above source as a symptom of a

basilar skull fracture. The term of "Raccoon Eyes" wasn't used in the story as unclear if this term was in use in 1896. Also, the description of the fluid (its colour and location) on Miss Newman's ear. Dr Locke's intention to examine Miss Newman's brain is based upon known effects basilar skull fractures may have on the brain as outlined in the above source. Any examination Dr Locke makes would be in search of general damage rather than to check for the specific diagnosis outlined in the above source, though.

Zinfandel Wine Grapes, Flavor, Character, History, Wine Food Pairing article on the Wine Cellar Insider website
https://www.thewinecellarinsider.com/wine-topics/wine-educational-questions/grapes-for-wine-making-flavor-characteristics-explained/zinfandel-wine-grapes-flavor-character-history/
Reference to the colour of the fluid on Miss Newman's ear resembling zinfandel wine made by Dr Locke; comparison taken directly from p.65 of the BODY TRAUMA book (see full source information above). The Zinfandel wine article used to establish the origins and availability of this wine in 1896 so that Dr Locke could reference it in the story.

The Case of the Impossible Implication

May, Trevor, The Victorian Public School (2009, Shire Publications, Great Britain)
The general workings of Victorian public schools, teaching & learning, and the life of a schoolboy.

***

The following sources are from the British Newspaper Archive website:

Illustrated Sporting and Dramatic News **Published in 1896.**
https://www.britishnewspaperarchive.co.uk/titles/illustrated-sporting-and-dramatic-news
Reference to the publication being in Mr Waller's bedroom.

Sporting Times **Published in 1896.**
https://www.britishnewspaperarchive.co.uk/titles/sporting-times
Reference to the publication being in Mr Waller's bedroom.

The Case of the Lyall Lighthouse

CARLISLE, DUMFRIES, KILMARNOCK and GLASGOW section of Bradshaw's Rail Times for Great Britain and Ireland. December 1895. p.546
The departure time, location, and nature of the Bow Street Society members' train to Scotland.

McCloskey, Keith, The Lighthouse: The Mystery of the Eilean Mor Lighthouse Keepers (2014, The History Press; Illustrated edition, England)
The connection between Robert Louis Stevenson and the Northern Lighthouse Board (NLB).
Northern Lighthouse Board covering lighthouses in Scotland & the Isle of Man, Trinity House covering lighthouses in England & the Channel Islands, and Irish Lights covering lighthouses in Eire and Northern Ireland.
Also, the Irish Lights head office being in Dublin and the Northern Lighthouse Board's address in Edinburgh.
The roles and duties of the lightkeepers, and Superintendent Roy's position and duties.

General background information about lighthouse management and construction in Scotland in the nineteenth century.

The Case of the Bold Blackmailer

The following sources are from the *Living Archive* website:
https://www.livingarchive.org.uk

***The Wolverton to Stony Stratford Tramway* article:**
https://www.livingarchive.org.uk/content/local-history/areas/wolverton/the-wolverton-to-stony-stratford-tramway#:~:text=The%20Wolverton%20to%20Stony%20Stratford%20tramway%20was%20opened%20in%201887,it%20proved%20uneconomic%20to%20operate.
The existence, route, and the description of the appearance of the Wolverton to Stony Stratford steam tramway.

***Wolverton Station from the car park – Wolverton September 1988* image. Reference number BSC/002/025:**
https://www.livingarchive.org.uk/content/catalogue_item/the-bill-skeats-collection/views-of-wolverton/wolverton-station-from-the-car-park
The description of three covered stairways and exterior of the building.

***Wolverton Station booking hall – Wolverton September 1988* image. Reference number BSC/002/024:**
https://www.livingarchive.org.uk/content/catalogue_item/the-bill-skeats-collection/views-of-wolverton/wolverton-station-booking-hall
The description of the interior of the train station.

***

The following sources are from the *Wolverton Past Blog*:
http://wolvertonpast.blogspot.com

19th Century Station Masters article.
http://wolvertonpast.blogspot.com/2012/06/19th-century-stationmasters.html
The owner of Wolverton Works and the train station. Also, the existence of a station master.

Wolverton in its Prime - 1 The Works article, specifically the 1905 map of Wolverton Works.
https://wolvertonpast.blogspot.com/2011/05/wolverton-in-its-prime-1-works.html
Location of the works, the streets, and tram route.

The Third Station article, specifically the photograph and accompanying description of the white train station built in 1881 and demolished circa 1990.
https://wolvertonpast.blogspot.com/2010/12/third-station.html?m=1
Location of the station and the interior and exterior descriptions of it.

The Case of the Cryptic Clues

The following sources are from the *Historic England* website:

Listing entry for 28-36, Hyde Vale SE10
https://historicengland.org.uk/listing/the-list/list-entry/1078969?section=official-list-entry
The date the Mirrells' house was built.

Image of 34, Hyde Vale: Record No 63990 Title: House in Hyde Vale Description: View of front elevation of

house at 34 Hyde Vale, Greenwich. Date of execution: 1964.
https://www.londonpicturearchive.org.uk/view-item?i=66235&WINID=1695556468057
Appearance of the Mirrells' house.

***

Charles Booth's London Poverty maps and police notebooks
https://booth.lse.ac.uk/
Locations of Hyde Vale, Royal Naval College, Greenwich Station, and Greenwich Park. Also, the names given to these in 1898.

William Dunbar **biography on the Encyclopaedia Britannica website**
www.britannica.com/biography/William-Dunbar
The name and origins of the term "The Thrissill and the Rois" quoted by Miss Trent.

Royal Naval College opens at Greenwich – 1 February 1873 **article from the** ***Old Royal Navy College*** **website.**
https://ornc.org/news/rnc-opens/#:~:text=The%20Royal%20Naval%20College%20fi nally,lowered%20for%20the%20last%20time.
Gunnery lieutenants, sub-lieutenants, and their training.

An Act to amend the Laws relating to the Government of the Navy. [28th August 1860.] **AKA the Navy Act 1860.**
Crimes and punishments within the navy mentioned in the story.

Printed in Great Britain
by Amazon

41779228R00091